John Joseph Curran

Golden Jubilee of the Reverend Fathers Dowd and Toupin

With Historical Sketch of Irish Community of Montreal

John Joseph Curran

Golden Jubilee of the Reverend Fathers Dowd and Toupin
With Historical Sketch of Irish Community of Montreal

ISBN/EAN: 9783744741064

Printed in Europe, USA, Canada, Australia, Japan

Cover: Foto ©Raphael Reischuk / pixelio.de

More available books at **www.hansebooks.com**

GOLDEN JUBILEE

OF THE

REVEREND FATHERS

DOWD AND TOUPIN,

WITH

HISTORICAL SKETCH OF IRISH COMMUNITY
OF MONTREAL.

BIOGRAPHIES OF PASTORS OF "RECOLLET"
AND "ST. PATRICK'S," ETC.

EDITED BY

J. J. CURRAN, Q.C., M.P.

Montreal:
PRINTED BY JOHN LOVELL & SON.
1887.

INDEX.

LIST OF SUBSCRIBERS

TO THE

JUBILEE CELEBRATION FUND OF REV. FATHER DOWD.

FOR THE REDUCTION OF THE DEBT ON ST. PATRICKS CHURCH.

Assetts, Mrs	$5 00	Clifford, Daniel	20 00
Ahern, Ann	1 00	Clifford, Denis	20 00
Ahern, John	3 00	Callaghan, John, sen	20 00
Ahern, Ellen	5 00	Corbett, Patrick	10 00
Anderson, J. T	10 00	Clifford, John	10 00
Alty, Thomas	4 00	Cummings, Mrs. George	5 00
Brannan, J. B	50 00	Callahan, Michael	5 00
Barry, John	40 00	Chambers, John	5 00
Byrne, Miss R	25 00	Carroll, Jane	10 00
Bermingham, John	20 00	Cullen, Margaret	5 00
Burress, Widow	5 00	Cafferty, Paul	5 00
Barron, Denis	5 00	Carroll, Daniel	5 00
Brady, Widow	4 00	Conway, Widow Alice	25 00
Bradley, Mrs	2 00	Callaghan, John, jun	5 00
Brennan, Thomas	5 00	Collins, Thos. C	50 00
Buchanan, Thomas	50 00	Callaghan, James	5 00
Brosnan, Bridget	2 00	Cuddihy, Widow Michael	25 00
Breen, John	5 00	Carroll, Margaret	6 00
Burns, Michael	5 00	Connolly, Wm	10 00
Behan, Thomas	10 00	Connolly, Jas., jun	5 00
Brennan, Edward	2 00	Collins, John	5 00
Bully, Mrs. Wm	1 00	Chanteloup, E	25 00
Burke, Mary	2 00	Carr, Emma	0 75
Byrne, Thomas	2 00	Coolahan, Sarah	1 00
Beaudry, Widow	10 00	Cassidy, Cath	1 00
Booth, William	10 00	Connolly, Sarah	1 00
Barbeau, E. J	25 00	Cluin, John	10 00
Barbeau, Henry	10 00	Cross, Samuel	5 00
Bantree, Harvey	5 00	Conway, James	20 00
Brennan, Arthur	20 00	Cunningham, Catherine	10 00
Cunningham, W. H	100 00	Cunningham, Mary Ann	10 00
Carroll, Michael	100 00	Callahan, Mrs. Felix	10 00
Christy, T	50 00	Connolly, John	5 00
Curran, J. J., M.P	50 00	Campbell, Cassie	2 00
Crowe, John	50 00	Collins, James	40 00
Conaughton, James	25 00	Coyle, P. J	25 00

A

Costello, Ellen	1 00	Dooner, Mrs. George	5 00
Cunnis, Mrs. John	1 00	Duff, Ann	1 00
Cannon, Miss Ann	8 00	Dunn, John	25 00
Clarke, John	2 00	Durack, Widow Patrick	15 00
Callaghan, Johanna	2 00	Dillon, J. T	5 00
Cuddy, Michael	5 00	Dillon, J. St. G	10 00
Curran, John	25 00	Dillon, R. Lacy	5 00
Creamer, W	5 00	Dillon, Frank	5 00
Clifford, Widow John	19 72	Donnelly, Theresa	3 00
Carroll, James	25 00	Donnelly, James	5 00
Carroll, Joseph	5 00	Dunn, James	20 00
Collection May 19th	155 18	Dillon, Frederick	3 00
Callery, James	5 00	Dunning, Widow Jas	5 00
Connaughton, Margaret	2 00	Dowling, Michael	10 00
Carroll, Philip	5 00	Downey, Mrs. Nora	2 00
Clayton, John	10 00	Delaney, Mrs	5 00
Callahan, Felix	10 00	Elliott Edward	100 00
Coghlin, B. J	50 00	Emerson, Bernard	10 00
Calgay, Mrs	1 00	Edwards, Joseph	5 00
Clifford, Mrs. Daniel	10 00	Egginton, Jos. A	20 00
Cass, Mrs. Widow	10 00	Egan, Michael	2 00
Cunningham, Thomas	5 00	Egan, Patrick	5 00
Dwane, John	100 00	Elliott, Martin	50 00
Delahanty, Michael	50 00	Enright, Widow John	2 00
Doherty, Charles J	50 00	Egan, Mary	2 00
Doran, William E	50 00	Fogarty, Jeremiah	100 00
Dunlop, James	10 00	Feron, Michael	50 00
Daly, Thomas	10 00	Foley, Jeremiah	50 00
Dunlop, B	5 00	Fallon, John	25 00
Drury, Widow	2 00	Furlong, Mrs. Anne	10 00
Devins, R. J	100 00	Finnan, Bridget	1 00
Duffy, J. J	20 00	Friend, A	1 00
Duggan, Rev. John, Water-		Friend, A	5 00
bury, Conn., U.S	25 00	Feron, Widow Arthur	2 00
Doran, William	100 00	Fox, John	2 00
Dredge, Annie	5 00	Friend, A	10 00
Dowd, Francis	20 00	Friend, A	50 00
Dwyer, John	5 00	Friend, A	1 00
Doyle, Patrick (baker)	25 00	Fogarty, Timothy Frs	100 00
Downs, Terence	5 00	Friend, A	1 00
Drake, Richard	5 00	Friend, A	10 00
Dowling, William	20 00	Friend, A	10 00
Drumm, Francis	10 00	Fitzgerald, Mary	1 00
Dillon, Ned	5 00	Friend, A	10 00
Doherty, Hon. Justice	125 00	Friend, A	2 00
Daly, Bridget	1 00	Friend, A	3 00

Friend, A	10 00	Friends, Two	2 00
Fogarty, Patrick	2 00	Fowler, Prof. J. A	20 00
Friends, Three	3 00	Friend, A	2 00
Friend, A	5 00	Friend, A	0 50
Friends, Three	3 00	Friend, A	5 00
Friend, A	5 00	Friend, A	5 00
Friend, A	1 00	Foley, Mrs. Jeremiah	5 00
Foley, Ann and Winifred	5 00	Friend, A	1 00
Friend, A	100 00	Friend, A	375 00
Flood, Mary	2 00	Friend, A	1 50
Feeney, Cath	6 00	Flynn, Mrs. Lawrence	5 00
Friend, A	1 00	Grant, George R	100 00
Friend, A	2 00	Griffin, Widow	5 00
Friend, A	1 00	Gorrie, Michael	5 00
Friend, A	1 00	Gleeson, Bridget	10 00
Friend, A (per Father Toupin,		Gaherty, John	5 00
name forgotten)	5 00	Grace, Patrick	100 00
Ferguson, Thos	5 00	Groome, P. M	25 00
Friend, A	5 00	Gorman, Michael	10 00
Falton, Martin	4 00	Gilligan, John	5 00
Farrell, Widow John	5 00	Gunning, Bernard	5 00
Friend, A	2 00	Green, Thomas	10 00
Friend, A	1 00	Gallagher, Widow Patrick	25 00
Fayer, Miss	0 50	Grubert, Lawrence	10 00
Flanagan, M. M. J	10 00	George, W., (surname forgotten)	4 86
Funchion, Mary	1 00	Geherty, Denis (Carillon)	5 00
Friend, A	2 00	Hingston, Dr. W. H	250 00
Friend, A	1 00	Hodson, William H	50 00
Fitzgerald, Thomas	5 00	Hewitt, Thomas	4 00
Finn, Timothy	5 00	Hamill, Patrick, jun	2 00
Friend, A	3 00	Hamill, Patrick, sen	2 00
Farrell, Mrs. Wm	5 00	Hearn, Ann	2 00
Friend, A	1 50	Hamilton, Widow John	2 00
Friend, A	1 00	Hughes, Michael, sergt	15 00
Friend, A	2 00	Hart, Martin	25 00
Friend, A	2 00	Hallinan, John	3 00
Friend, A	10 00	Heaney, Widow	2 00
Friend, A	0 25	Harris —	1 00
Friend, A	5 00	Harris, Arthur	1 00
Fallon, Rev. P	25 00	Hart, Widow Martin	10 00
Friend, A	2 00	Hackett, Widow James	2 00
Friend, A	1 00	Harvey, Thomas	10 00
Friend, A	1 00	Hughes, Louis	30 00
Friend, A	0 25	Hayvern, John	2 00
Farrell, William	50 00	Hetherson, Mary	4 00
Fitzpatrick, Jane	5 00	Hunt, John J	4 00

Name	Amount	Name	Amount
Hart, O. and E	50 00	Lyc s, Bridget	5 00
Hassett, Mrs. Thos	10 00	Logue, Jane	5 00
Holland, Mrs. Thos	2 00	Lynch, Michael	2 00
Heagarty, John	25 00	Lawless, Marcella	31 75
Harrington, Mary	20 00	Loye, Francis	5 00
Hanton, Mary	1 00	Lovit, Mrs	5 00
Irwin, Edward	100 0	Laverty, M. P	10 00
Irwin, Eddy D	10 0	Laverty, Mrs. Joseph	2 00
Irwin, Mary Eleanor	10 00	Laforce, Mrs. Widow	5 00
Irwin, Walter Patrick	10 00	Murphy, Edward	1000 00
Irwin, Katy	10 00	Murphy, John D	1000 00
Irwin, Frank Bartley	10 00	Mullin, James E	500 00
Irwin, Ethel Clare	10 00	Milloy, J. J	100 00
Ivery, Widow James	4 00	Mullin, Widow John	50 00
Jones, Widow	0 50	Menzies, Augustus	50 00
Johnston, Anastasia	1 00	Maloney, Michael	25 00
Jensen John L	100 00	Moore, Mary Ann	25 00
Johnston, Mrs	1 00	Massett, Robert	12 00
Kavanagh, Michael	250 00	Marshall, Miss	1 00
Kelly, Patrick	100 00	Murphy, James	5 00
Kavanagh, Walter	100 00	Martin, Patrick	20 00
Kennedy, Mrs. John	5 00	Muldoon, Patrick Neil	3 00
Kennedy, Catherine	5 00	Moynaugh, Patrick	20 00
Kennedy, Janet	5 00	Mullin, Daniel	50 00
Kelly, Mary	2 00	Moran, Edward	25 00
Kelly, Mary (another)	2 00	Murphy, Patrick	5 00
Kennedy, John	5 00	Marshall, Miss Ann	5 00
Ker, Thomas	25 00	Murren, Henry	5 00
Kelly, William	5 00	Mansfield, Richard	5 00
Kehoe, Patrick	5 00	Morley, Michael	50 00
Kavanagh. Mary	3 00	Mullin, Patrick	100 00
Kiernan, William	5 00	Mulcair, Bros	50 00
Kitty, Mrs	5 00	Murphy, Ann	4 00
Kelly, Mrs	5 00	Morgan, Edward	2 00
Kirby, Patrick	5 00	Maddock, Patrick	4 00
Kinsella, James	10 00	Moore, Mrs	5 00
Kennedy, J. G	20 00	Mullin, Thomas	10 00
Kennedy, N	10 00	Maher, Bridget	5 00
Kennedy, Patrick	100 00	Mathews, Patrick	5 00
Kane, Sarah	5 00	Malone, Ellen	5 00
Kiely Richard	5 00	Morrissey, Thomas	5 00
Kenehan, James	5 00	Murphy, Mrs. Ed. (St. Jos. St.	5 00
Kavanagh, Henry	30 00	Murphy, James	5 00
Kenny, Bridget	1 00	Murphy, Patrick Edw	5 00
Lanning, J. J	25 00	Malone, Ann	10 00
Love, T. H	100 00	Mullarkey, Michael	50 00

Malone, Kate	3 00	McGuire, Julia	5 00
Maher, Mrs. Terence	5 00	McHenry, Miss Isabella	5 00
Main, James	20 00	McQuilken, Mrs	2 00
McGarvey, Owen	1000 00	McKeown, Patrick	10 00
McCready, James	500 00	McNally, Bernard	50 00
McShane, (Hon.) James	200 00	McKenna, Patrick (florist)	10 00
McEntyre, Daniel	100 00	McCabe, Mary	2 43
McEntyre, John	100 00	McDonald, Elizabeth	5 00
McCrory, P	1 00	McDonald, Emily	5 00
McGoldrick, P	50 00	McDonald, Janet	1 00
McAndrew, M. J	25 00	McDonough, John	5 c
McAnally, R	25 00	McCaffrey, Dennis	10 00
McCarthy, Callaghan	10 00	McGuire, James	5 00
McInerney, John	10 00	McManus, Mary Ann	5 00
McDonald, Mary	5 00	McNulty, Elizabeth	5 00
McCarthy, Mrs	1 00	McCarthy, Rev. Father	50 00
McDonald, Emily	1 00	McDonald, Maggie	2 00
McBrarty, John	5 00	McDonnell, Ann	1 00
McClanagan, D	50 00	McGuire, Wm	4 00
McDermott, Widow	25 00	Macdonald, Dr. J. A	10 00
McDonald, Daniel	2 00	McCurragh, Isabella	20 00
McKenna, Widow Thos	10 00	McCormack, Widow Michael	5 00
McCready, Widow Robt	25 00	McPherson, A	5 00
McNama	2 00	McDonald, Margaret	2 00
McMahon J. W	3 00	McCrory, Joseph	25 00
McAran, James	10 00	McPhail, Elizabeth	2 00
McCarthy, James	5 00	McGarr, Michael	5 00
McCarthy, Mrs. Elizabeth	2 00	McKenzie, John	10 00
McLaughlin, Miss Ann	40 00	Nugent, J. P	50 00
McCormack, Maggie	1 00	Nelligan, Patrick	10 00
McFee, Mrs	1 00	Nugent, James	5 00
McCall, Philip	5 00	Nolan, Charles	2 00
McMahon, Ellen	3 00	Nolan, John	2 00
McCulloch, Miss Mary	10 00	Nibbs, Mrs	5 00
McCall, Edward	10 00	Nolan, Julia	5 00
McCann, Joseph	5 00	Newman, Mrs	1 00
McMahon, Michael	10 00	O'Brien, James	1000 00
McCarthy, Wm	5 00	O'Hara, William J	500 00
McDonald, Ann	1 00	O'Connor, James	10 00
McDonnell, Mrs. John	4 00	O'Sullivan, Florence	3 00
McCready, Michael	50 00	O'Shaughnessy, M	10 00
McGreevy, Patrick	10 00	O'Neil, Cath	2 00
McCabe, Patrick	15 00	O'Sullivan, Mrs. Margt	5 00
McDonald, Kate	5 00	O'Connell, Michael	10 00
McDonald, Lizzie	5 00	O'Loughlin, Martin J	10 00
McCaffrey, Mrs. Margaret	5 00	O'Neil, Patrick	10 00

O'Leary, John	5 00	Shea, Jeremiah	10 00
O'Neil, T. J	5 00	Sinnett, D	5 00
O'Reilly, Bernard	2 00	Sinnett, Mrs	5 00
O'Sullivan, Michael	10 00	Stuart, Mrs	1 00
O'Brien, Mrs. T	5 00	Smith, Patrick	5 00
O'Brien, Patrick	10 00	Sadlier, Mrs	25 00
O'Shaughnessy, James	10 00	Sadlier, James A	200 00
O'Neil, D	10 00	Servant girl, A	1 00
Phelan, M	50 00	Semple, J. H	200 00
Potts, John	25 00	Servants, Two	2 00
Power, Bridget, widow	2 00	Sharkey, James	3 00
Powers, Misses	5 00	Stapleton, Miss Mary	5 00
Platt, — (Plateau St)	4 00	Smith, Chas. F	100 00
Pendergast, Ann	5 00	Sheridan, Wm. Patrick	5 00
Pendergast, Mary	2 00	Sharkey, Ellen	5 00
Power, Widow Richard	2 00	Scanlan, Mrs	5 00
Price, Martin	5 00	Scullion, Edward	5 00
Parishioner, A	5 00	Stark, Patrick	6 00
Phelan, D	50 00	Sibbins, Mary Ann	1 00
Quinn, Michael	100 00	Silhy, William	4 00
Quipp, J. E. H	10 00	Sharkey, Michael	10 00
Quinn, Widow Mary	5 00	Sheppard, Jonathan	1 00
Quelch, Ellen	2 00	Starr, Timothy	10 00
Quinn, Widow James	5 00	Starr, Mrs. Christina	10 00
Ryan, Hon. Thomas	1000 00	Symmons, Mrs	4 00
Ryan, M. P	500 00	Smith, Widow Bridget	5 00
Reiplinger, John	50 00	Sparks, Misses	5 00
Reynolds, P	25 00	Scullion, H. M	2 00
Rawley, Richard	20 00	Servant girl, A	50 00
Redmond, Widow	20 00	Stewart, Wm	2 00
Reilly, Jane	10 00	Servants, Two	4 00
Reilly, William	25 00	Smith, James	0 50
Ryan, Mrs. Patrick	10 00	Stack, Edward	10 00
Rowell, Mrs	5 00	Shea, John S	2 00
Reilly, Thos. (Vallée St.)	100 00	Smith, James H	2 00
Ryan, widow Michael	10 00	Slavin, Agnes	2 00
Ryan, Hon. Thos. and Mrs. (2nd)	50 00	Tansey, Bernard	100 00
Ronayne, Edw. P	25 00	Tiffin, Widow Thos	100 00
Routh, Widow	2 00	Tierney, Henry	5 00
Ryan, Elizabeth	100 00	Toomey, John	1 00
Rowan, Peter	10 00	Trumble, Mrs. Margaret	1 00
Ryan, Catherine	1 25	Tansey, James	5 00
Rabaut, Chas. P. (Detroit)	20 00	Thompson, The Hon. Mr.	
Roerty, Julia	1 00	(Minister of Justice)	20 00
Rutledge, Mary	5 00	Todd, Ann	1 00
Styles, Thomas	20 00	Wright, P	100 00

Wright, Michael	50 00	Wall, Joseph	5 00
Waddell, Thomas H.	20 00	Wall, James (Donegann St.).	50 00
Waddell, Henry	10 00	Wilson, William	20 00
Whelan, Widow Edw	5 00	Ward, William	2 00
Walsh, Julia	2 00	Ward, Henry J	10 00
Warnock, M'ss Ellen	2 00	Watt, Ellen	5 00
Waddell, Mrs. T. H	10 00	Walsh, Widow Michael	20 00
Wall, Henry	5 00	Whelan, Widow Ann	100 00
Wood, Arthur	5 00	Walsh, Catherine	5 00
Walsh, James Jos	3 00	Whelan, Widow John	5 00
Warren, Robt. (Mayor St)	20 00	Whelan, John P	500 00
Wall, Thomas	5 00	Wallace, John	2 00
Wall, Thos., jun	5 00		

SOCIETIES.

St. Patrick's Society	$100 00	Living Rosary	251 25
" Choir	230 00	Children of Catechism	544 25
" School (girls).	300 00	Cath. Young Men's Society	205 00
Ex-pupils, St. Patrick's Sch.		Leo Club	106 49
(girls)	65 00	Children of Mary	200 00
St. Patrick's T. A. & B.Soc.	500 00	Orphans, Relatives of	50 00
Ladies of Charity and friends.	1000 00	Non-Catholic friends	387 00

RISE AND PROGRESS
OF THE
IRISH CATHOLIC COMMUNITY
IN THE
CITY OF MONTREAL AND VICINITY.

HE 19th day of May, 1887, will long be remembered by the citizens of Montreal, and more especially by the Irish Catholic worshippers at the shrine of Saint Patrick. It was truly a great day, great for the city because its celebration called forth Christian sentiments of brotherly love amongst all classes and creeds in the community, evoked by a feeling of admiration for a lifetime spent in the practice of heroic virtues ; great for those specially committed to the charge of the venerable Pastor whose Jubilee was being held because of the magnificent results it has already produced and those that are likely to flow from it in the early future.

A narrative of the many forms in which the gratitude of a people to a beloved pastor, and one of his most zealous associates, honoring together the 50th anniversary of the day on which they consecrated themselves to the service of the Most High, and were ordained His priests for ever, would form a neat little memento of so auspicious an event ; yet we may be permitted to make of that day an epoch, in another sense, and choose it as the point from which to glance at the history of the congregation engaged in its celebration. To-day the position of the Irish Catholic community of Montreal and its vicinity is one of influence, power and prestige. The assessment rolls are evidence of the interest they command to the extent of millions of dollars. Their hold on commerce and manufactures, their representation in the Judiciary, in

the Senate and Commons of the Dominion, in the Local Legis-
lature, at the Aldermanic board, in the various offices of trust
and emolument connected with public affairs and their place
in the learned professions, by men of their race and creed,
leave no room for cavil. Census returns are scarcely needed
to establish numerical strength, when not only the throngs
that worship at St. Patrick's from early morn until noon at
the successive masses, but the congregations of Saint Ann
and Saint Anthony, Saint Gabriel and Saint Mary m. be
viewed every Sunday, and are the living evidence of how
the Irish Catholic population of this great and growing city
have increased and multiplied and preserved the inestimable
boon of the faith of their fathers. With all this in view, and
other unmistakeable signs of moral and material progress,
can it be realized that only a few years ago the Irish Catholics
of Montreal were so mere a handful as not even to attract
notice to their existence, and that it was only in 1817 a
zealous priest of Saint Sulpice learned that a small colony
of the sons and daughters of the Green Isle were to be met
every Sunday, pouring forth their supplication to God at the
shrine of His Immaculate Mother, *Notre Dame de Bonsecours.*
It was but natural they should have flocked there, their lively
faith was intensified by their isolation in a strange land, and
the sequel shows that they appealed not in vain for the protection of Our Lady of Good Help. In 1817 the Rev. Father
Richards of the S· S. discovered this little band of Irish
Catholic worshippers, numbering not more than from 30 to
50 adults. They increased but slowly, since in a directory
of the city published in 1819 we find not more than 30 names
that could be identified as hailing from Ireland, and in 1820
their number was still so small that a prominent gentleman
who visited the Bonsecours church in that year stated, " he
" could have covered with a good sized parlor carpet all the
" Irish Catholics worshipping there on Sundays." The tide
of immigration soon set in, and in 1830, the congregation
had largely increased. At that time the old " Recollet "

church on Notre Dame street was considerably enlarged, and in the following year was reopened for the use of the Irish Catholics of the centre and western portion of the city, those of the eastern section still remaining attached to *Notre Dame de Bonsecours.* From that time until the opening of St. Patrick's the Recollet was the religious head-quarters of the Irish Catholics of Montreal. There the Rev. Father, afterwards Bishop, Phelan commenced his most remarkable career of usefulness as pastor of our people.

The indefatigable Father Richards still continued his labors in the interest of the section of the community to which he was so devotedly attached. In 1829 the church of Notre Dame, commonly known amongst the English speaking residents of Montreal to this day as the "French Church," was opened. There the Rev. Father gathered the Irish soldiers in the British Garrison then stationed here every Sunday morning at eight o'clock mass, and numbers of Irish Catholic civilians unable to attend morning service at the "Recollet," used to flock and assist at the holy sacrifice at the Virgin's Altar when a short but impressive sermon was invariably preached. The contingent from Ireland swelled to large proportions in 1831-32, and the "Recollet" became altogether inadequate to the wants of the people. Not only was the sacred edifice crammed to suffocation at High Mass, but across Notre Dame street and in Dollard lane, opposite to the line of St. James street, the devout worshippers actually knelt in the road way in rain or sunshine.

This rapid increase necessarily gave rise to a demand for further accommodation, and room had to be found for the Irish who could not attend Mass at the Recollet, and crowded the low masses in Notre Dame, Bonsecours and other churches. Rev. Father Patrick Phelan, who was ordained in 1825, continued his pastorate at the Recollet Church till his consecration as co-adjutor Bishop of Kingston in 1843. His successor was Rev. J. J. Connolly. The relief came at last. After several meetings of the Irish Catholics, in which urgent representations were made to the Seminary and Fabrique on the absolute necessity of a new church, the Fabrique determined upon building one which should bear the title of their patron St. Patrick. In this consummation they were efficaciously assisted by the Abbe Quiblier, Superior of the Seminary of St. Sulpice, who held the Irish in high esteem, with full appreciation of their services to the cause of religion, in consequence of which he strongly supported their claims in the premises.

No time was lost ; on the 20th May, 1843, the purchase of the land was made, comprising the area bounded by Lagauchetiere, St. Alexander and Dorchester streets (including the sites of St. Patrick's Orphan Asylum and St. Bridget's Home and Night Refuge, the property was bought of the Rocheblave family for £5,000 or $20,000. Shortly afterwards the ground was broken and blessed by the Bishop of Montreal and a cross was planted according to usage. Immediately the work of digging the foundation was begun, and on the 26th of September of the same year, the corner stones were blessed and laid. They were seven in number ; they were blessed by the Bishop, Monseigneur Ig. Bourget, and laid by the following :—1st by the Bishop, 2nd by the Mayor, 3rd Speaker of House of Assembly, 4th by Chief Justice, 5th by President Irish Temperance Association, 6th by President St. Patrick's Society, 7th by President Hibernian Benevolent Society.

The work was prosecuted with vigor, through the zealous efforts of the Fabrique, under the superintendence of Messrs. Compte & Marr, and all the materials employed were of the most desirable and substantial character. Finally, on the 17th March, 1847, the church was dedicated to the honor of St. Patrick, and the inauguration partook largely of the ceremonial generally observed on the festival of the patron Saint of Ireland. Early in the morning of that day, all the Irish Societies comprising the St. Patrick's Society, the Hibernian Benevolent Society and the Irish Catholic Temperance

Society, with the children of the Christian Brothers attached to the Recollet Church, and the whole body of the Irish Catholics of the city, joined in grand procession, accompanied by banners and bands at the Recollet Church, on Notre Dame street, and marched to the Place d'Armes, where they were joined by the Bishop of Montreal and a number of the clergy of Notre Dame and others, whom the societies conducted to the new church. The attendance of clergy and laity was so large that the sacred edifice was packed to the doors. High Mass was celebrated by Right Rev. J. C. Prince, coadjutor of the Bishop of Montreal, assisted by a number of gentlemen of the Seminary. The eloquent sermon on the occasion was preached by Rev. J. J. Connolly, director of the Irish Catholics of Montreal, to the text: "Build the house and it shall be acceptable to me. I shall be glorified." The further success of the demonstration may be gathered from the collection taken up at mass, amounting to £53 or $212, a large sum for those times. After the celebration of the Holy Sacrifice, the procession was reformed and paraded the street, according to the custom on St. Patrick's Day.

Father Connolly continued to preside over the fortunes of the new church and parish until 1860, when he resigned and it became necessary to find his successor. Several years before, in 1846, very Rev. M. Quiblier, superior of the Seminary, who always remained the staunch friend of the Irish Catholics, had visited Ireland expressly to recruit priests for them, and obtained permission from the then Primate of all Ireland, the Most Rev. Dr. Crolly, for the transfer to Montreal of Revs. Fathers Dowd, O'Brien, McCullough and others, all of them distinguished for their piety, zeal and eloquence, while Fathers Dowd and O'Brien were further noted for their great administrative abilities. The choice of a new pastor was therefore an easy task, and Father Dowd, appointed by the Seminary, entered upon those duties which he has discharged uninterruptedly for the past 27 years.

The year 1847 was further painfully memorable for the

Irish Catholics of Montreal in the outbreak and ravages of typhus fever. A few months after the opening of St. Patrick's Church, a number of the clergy of St. Sulpice contracted the pestilence, while attending the poor Irish immigrants at the fever sheds, Point St. Char'es, where the pastor, Father Connolly, had distinguished himself by his zeal and great labors among the infected, and several of these devoted men died the death of martyrs, among them being the venerable Father Richards and Father Morgan, a cousin of Father Dowd, who had preceded him to Canada by a few years, and several others. In consequence of this great mortality, the Seminary secured the aid of five Jesuit Fathers, just arrived in the country, and for a few years these assisted in the ministry of St. Patrick's until the Seminary found means to do the work once more through its own members. The more recent history of the congregation is fresh in the minds of all who feel an interest therein. One of its pleasing features was the pilgrimage to Rome headed by the Rev. Father Dowd in 1877 when the good priest had the pleasure of laying at the feet of Pope Pius IX. the sum of $6,000 as the contribution of his parishioners to His Holiness.

A brief sketch of the new parish of St. Patrick's under the late parochial distribution will be found in another part of this little volume. As already mentioned, the parishes of St. Ann and St. Anthony, St. Gabriel and St. Mary each have their large contingent of the Irish Catholic population of the City of Montreal, but all look up to the venerable pastor of St. Patrick's as the father of the Irish Catholic people of this city and district. His career proves him to have been a Providential man. Coming at a critical moment in our people's history, he has guided their steps and unceasingly watched and unflinchingly contended for their interests. They were growing in number but lacking the institutions necessary to consolidation ; these his great powers of administration have provided. His like we may never see again, but the influence of his master mind will be felt long after the call shall have gone forth

14

summoning him to the eternal reward of his arduous labors.
The Irish Catholics of Montreal will ever look to St. Patrick's
as the great centre towards which all their general interests
converge. Animated by the zeal and formed in the school of
the venerable pastor, others will, in God's own time, be found
to carry out the broad and comprehensive policy he has so
wisely devised ; but Heaven grant that the day may be far
distant when our people shall be deprived of the inestimable
benefits that are daily being conferred upon them by the
powerful intellect and boundless sympathies of their ever
loving and beloved Father Dowd.

PRIESTS WHO DIED DURING THE TYPHUS. .

Rev. Father Morgan.   Rev. Father Richard.
   "   " Richards.   "   " McInerney.
Rev. Father Hudon, V.G.

Mayor Mills.

SISTERS.

M. Adeline Limoges (Novice).   M. Rose Barbeau.
M. Angelique Chevrefils.   M. Alodie Bruyère (Postulant).
Janet Collins (Novice).   Charlotte Pominville.
M. Anne Nobles.

. of
ınd
so
far
ble
the

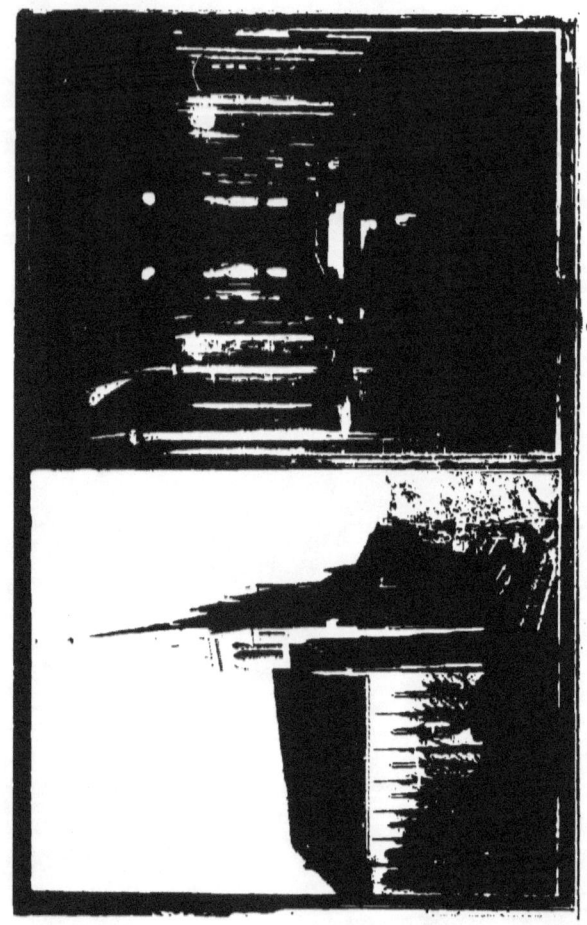

ST PATRICKS CHURCH
MONTREAL 1887.

ST. PATRICK'S CHURCH.

ST. PATRICK'S CHURCH is of the Gothic style of architecture of the 14th and 15th centuries. Its extreme length is 233ft and extreme width, 105ft. The foundation walls are 10ft thick and the height of the ceiling is 85ft. The height of the steeple is 228ft. The Church has three handsome and very appropriate altars—the main and two in the lateral chapels, and stained glass windows which are a highly effective ecclesiastical ornament. These altars were erected in place of the temporary shrines used before, and at the same date, the gilding, painting and ornamentation of the Church was done, and the stained glass also put in, by means of the voluntary subscriptions of the congregation, at a cost of between $40,000 to $50,000.

The acoustic properties of St. Patrick's are admirably adapted for preaching and music; and the organ, a gift of the congregation, has an excellent tone, while for size and volume it is well adapted to the requirements of the temple. There are two bells, having been chosen from four that formerly hung in the steeple of the old French Church or Notre Dame. The large one which was called *La Vieille Charlotte*, is of French make, and it is said like old bells generally, made in France, to have silver in its composition, which would account for it singularly fine tone. Little is known about the smaller bell, but it must be added that a third is much required, having the tone a pitch between the two. It is to be hoped that some member or members of the congregation will appreciate the need of completing the set by presenting this third bell to the Church.

NEW ST. PATRICK'S PARISH.

A small territory included within the following bounds was assigned to St. Patrick's, by the late Bishop Bourget, viz: bounded on the *East* by *Bleury* Street from *Craig* to *Sherbrooke* Streets, on the *North* by *Sherbrooke* from *Bleury* to Mountain Streets, on the *West* by *Mountain* from Sherbrooke to St. Antoine and *South* by St. Antoine and Craig to the corner of Bleury Street.

The French Canadians within this territory were to be parishioners of St. Patrick's ?

This state of things was not approved of by the Holy See—the system of national churches or by language was adopted as better suited to the mixed condition of the people. The English speaking Catholics, assigned by Bishop Bourget to St. Patrick's, Notre Dame and St. James, were attached as parishioners to St. Patrick's Church, and the territory of St. Patrick's now extends from *Mountain* Street to *Amherst* Street, *West* and *East* and from *Sherbrooke* Street to *William* Street, along William Street and down Grey n Street to the *River*, along the *River* front to Amherst, up Amherst to City *Boundary* and back by *St. Lawrence* and *Sherbrooke* to *Mour'n* St.

St. Patrick' Church has been distinguished from the beginning for the number and character of its religious, charitable, social and literary institutions, all of which have an extensive membership and are productive of good in many ways. Among these bodies are :—

St. Patrick's Total Abstinence Society.

The Scapular Society.	The Catholic Young Men's Society.
The Living Rosary.	The Leo Club.
The Ladies of Charity.	The Catechism Society.

Children of Mary.

The following are among the clergymen who officiated at different times in St. Patrick's Church since its opening in 1847 —

Rev. Father Richards.	Rev. Father O'Farrell (Now Bishop)
" " Connolly.	" " Brown.
" " O'Connell.	" " Bakewell.
" " Morgan.	" " Toupin.
" " McCullough	" " M. Callaghan.
" " MacMahon	" " J Callaghan.
" " Dowd.	" " Quinlivan.
" " O'Brien.	" " Singer.
" " Hogan.	" " Leclaire.

The present staff of the Church is :—

Rev. P. Dowd, Director,	Rev. M. Callaghan.
" M. Toupin.	" J. Callaghan.
" J. McCallen.	" J. Quinlivan.

ST. PATRICK'S ORPHAN ASYLUM.

THE terrible visitation of the typhus fever in 1847-48 was the immediate occasion of the establishment of an Orphan Asylum. A home became indispensable for the children whose parents fell victims, on th... arrival in Canada, to that fearful epidemic. The foundations of the Montreal St. Patrick's Orphan Asylum were laid in the fall of 1849, and the Institution was opened for the admission of children the 21st November, 1851. At a time when labor and materials were cheap, the building of the St. Patrick's Orphan Asylum cost nearly $20,000.00. This amount was promptly made up through subscriptions and collections, and a bequest of $4,000.00 left by the late Bartholomew O'Brien. In less than three months after the children first entered the Asylum all the building debt was paid.

The number of children admitted into the St. Patrick's Asylum since the beginning to the end of 1886 was 2436.

The average number in the house, at the same time, was 170. The average yearly cost of supporting the Institution is $10,000.00 The children of the Orphan Asylum are well prepared by a good education for a useful life in society, the little girls are trained in the house by the good Sisters ; the boys attend the schools of the Christian Brothers in the city. From the beginning the Asylum has been under the motherly care of the good Grey Nuns.

The Asylum is a civil Corporation, consisting of a Rev. Director and of ten Trustees.

One of the principal sources of revenue of the St. Patrick's Orphan Asylum has been the annual bazaar, under the auspices of the Ladies of St. Patrick's Congregation. In the follov ng letter from the pen of Mr. Edward Murphy (one of the Directors of the Institution), published orginally in " Le Bazaar " of the Cathedral, the details of the history of the Orphan's Bazaar are given and will be read with interest.

A REMARKABLE AND CREDITABLE RECORD.

HISTORY OF ST. PATRICK'S ORPHAN BAZAARS, FROM THEIR INCEPTION TILL 1885.

THE idea of a Bazaar, to be held each year for the support of the orphans of St. Patrick's Asylum, originated with a society of Irish ladies, belonging principally to the St. Patrick's congregation, in the year 1848. The first bazaar was held in October, 1849, in the St. Lawrence Hall, then newly built but not quite finished or occupied, which was k.. .., placed at the disposal of the Ladies of Charity by Mr. Corse, the owner, and a bazaar was held in the same month, with one exception, every year down to 1884. In 1885, it was not considered prudent to hold a bazaar on account of the great prevalence of smallpox. For that year the ladies provided for the wants of the orphans as best they could by collecting on their lists and holding their raffles in private. From 1849 to 1884, both years included, thirty-six (36) bazaars were held without interruption, and realized in the aggregate the very large sum of *one hundred and thirty-five thousand and ninety-nine dollars and thirty-six cents* (135,099.36.) This remarkable success is owing to the universal sympathy felt for the poor orphans, and which was shared in fully as much by Protestants as by Catholics. These bazaars, like many other good works, sprang from small beginnings, the first (in 1849) realized £130 ($520), the second (in 1850) realized £275 (1060), from which it grew up to a maximum of $5000 and over, at which sum it remained for many years, making the magnificent sum of over $135,000 in thirty-six years as seen above.

The society of Irish ladies that conducted the bazaar from year to year changed its lady president only *five* times during the whole period of thirty-seven (37) years. The names of these worthy presidents deserve to be recorded. The first was Mrs. Charles Wilson, Mdm. Vallière de St. Réal, Mrs. M. P. Ryan, Mrs. William Brennan, and the actual president, Mrs. Edward Murphy. In the case of all these ladies a gentle force had to be used to determine them to accept the honor of president. The fear lest the dear cause of charity should suffer in their refusal was common to all. Hence God blessed part, their labors, in which every member of the society took a willing and the work of charity continued to prosper in their united hands, because the true spirit of charity lived in their hearts, and kept them all together as one and the same family.

It must in justice be observed that for very many of these years the wonderful success of the St. Patrick's bazaars has been due, in no small measure, to the fostering care and heart warm encouragement of the venerable and beloved pastor of St. Patrick's, Rev. Father Dowd.

We are pleased to learn that the Ladies of Charity of St. Patrick's congregation, early in May last, unanimously resolved to postpone their annual bazaar for the orphans from October, the month it was

d in
ı884.
:ount
pro-
cting
49 to
:hout
ım of
and
ng to
ı was
"hese
.ings,
850)
5000
g the
ɔove.

year
vhole
ɔresi-
ilson,
ınan,
of all
ccept
ıarity
essed
illing
ands,
them

years
ue, in
ırage-
Rev.

rick's
tpone
t was

always held in, till November next, to allow the ladies of that parish full opportunity of working for St. Peter's Cathedral bazaar. We are happy to see that a large number of those ladies are working for that grand object, and we hope that in consideration of their having postponed the Orphans' Bazaar that they will be rewarded by the very general support of the benevolent to that most deserving charity.

EDW. MURPHY.

Montreal, 20th September, 1886.

ST. BRIDGET'S REFUGE.

THE St. Bridget's Refuge was opened for the admission of the poor in 1 65. It has a three-fold object;—to support old men and women; to give night-lodging to the destitute, without distinction of race or religion, and to protect female servants out of place. The cost of the building was $28,978.48, and of the first furniture outfit $4,186.37. The whole cost of building, and first outfit, was met by collections, except a bequest by Mr. Marsteller, of $6000.00 and a donation by the Seminary of $4,000.00.

From 1865 to 1886 inclusive, there was the following relief, given by the Refuge, viz :—

Night-lodgings with breakfast 203,461 thus divided :

To Catholics	171,852	
To Protestants	31,609	203,461

To Irish Catholics	154,160	
To French Canadians	30,169	
To English	14,767	
To Scotch	4,365	
		203,461

The average number of old infirm men and women in Refuge at same time 100.
The average number of servants placed out of Refuge yearly 300.
The average yearly cost of supporting Refuge $7,000 00.

The direction of the St Bridget's Refuge has always been under the care of the Grey Nuns. The Refuge is incorporated civilly; the corporation consists of a Rev. Director, a Rev. Vice-Director, and five Trustees.

ST. PATRICK'S GIRLS SCHOOL.

THE St. Patrick's School, separated from St. Patrick's Church by St. Alexander street, was built by the Seminary at a cost of nearly $30,000,00 for the little girls of St. Patrick's parish, and was first opened in 1872. It is conducted by the Sisters of Notre Dame. Its system of education is well digested, sound and practical, and bears good fruit every year in the superior training of the pupils who complete its course of studies. In forming the children, their future duties as house keepers are kept in view; hence knitting, plain sewing, mending, etc., are attended to as an essential part of their education.

The intellectual training of the children is of a high order, and marked by thorough solidity. Superficial teaching or study is not tolerated in the school. St. Patrick School is a blessing and an honor to St. Patrick's parish. The attendance is about five hundred.

RIGHT REVEREND BISHOP PHELAN.
FIRST PASTOR AT RECOLLET.

Father Patrick Phelan was one of the most zealous priests connected with the Irish Catholic population of the city of Montreal. For years he guided the people, and through the most turbulent period wisely directed their course. His name and memory will ever be dear to the descendants of the congregation he served so well. He was born in the Parish of Ballyragget, County Kilkenny, Ireland, and baptised on the 1st of February, 1795.

In a sketch of his life, published at Kingston in 1862," by the Clergymen who served Bishop Phelan's last mass " (printed by Lightfoot), we learn that before leaving Ireland as a student and teacher he had acquired the love and esteem of all who knew him; we are informed that " on the day of his departure not less than five hun. " dred persons of the Parish and vicinity assembled, through love " and respect, to convey him on his journey, and they accompanied " him as far as Castle Comer. Here, at the urgent request of Patrick " and his brother Daniel, they stopped and prepared to return, after " bidding a sorrowful farewell to one whom they esteemed so much. " His brother accompanied him to Dublin, whence Patrick deter- " mined to set sail for America. It so happened that the first ship " that was to put to sea was bound for Boston, and he, without fur-

" ther delay, took passage in her. On his arrival in Boston, he
" placed himself under the guardianship of Cardinal Cheverus, who,
" at that time, was Bishop of Boston. The Rev. William Taylor, of
" Boston, who had charge of transmitting to Montreal a copy of
" Patrick's exeat, informs us, in his letter of the 6th May, 1825,
" that, on his arrival at Boston, he presented himself to Bishop
" Cheverus, and was canonically adopted as a child of the Diocese
" of Boston. "

....

" Having remainded at Boston for three months, he was sent by
" Bishop Cheverus to the Seminary of Montreal to pursue his eccle-
" siastical studies. From his former conduct, we cannot but infer
" that these studies were scrupulously attended to, and that the three
" years which were to prepare him immediately for the Holy Minis-
" try found him giving his undivided attention to the sublime subjects
" which were propounded to him. On the 26th day of September,
" 1825, in the thirty-first year of his age, he received the Holy
" Order of Priesthood at the hands of Bishop Lartigue, first Bishop
" of Montreal. He was the first Priest ordained in the late Cathe-
" dral of St. James, Montreal, two days after its consecration, and the
" one thousand one hundred and sixty-first Priest whom Providence
" designed to labor in the Holy Ministry in Canada. His wishes
" were now fulfilled, and that long desired moment arrived which
" was to render him capable of effecting all the good which a heart
" like his desired. His zeal, notwithstanding all the difficulties he
" had to encounter in the course of his studies, did not in the least
" abate but rather increased. It soon became manifest that the
" young priest devoted himself so faithfully and successfully to his
" calling, that he endeared himself to all who had a knowledge of
" his labors. He did not fail to attract, before many weeks had
" elapsed, the attention of the Sulpician community ; and at the ear-
" nest solicitation of the Seminary of St. Sulpice, Bishop Cheverus
" allowed him to remain to administer to the wants of the Irish
" Catholics, who were emigrating to Canada, and fixing their abode
" at Montreal. According to Father Taylor, already mentioned, he
" merely departed to complete his studies in the Seminary of Mont-
" real, and had Bishop Cheverus' expressed permission to aggregate
" himself to the Sulpician community there. On the 21st day of
" November, of the same year of his ordination, he was received as a
" member of St. Sulpice, and he remained attached to the commu-

"nity, and serving the Irish congregation for nearly seventeen years,
"until shortly before he was called to the Episcopacy. "

....

Referring to the cholera which broke out with such violence
in 1832 and 1834 the biographer says:

"It was on this painful occasion that he truly showed himself the
"Priest of God and the people ; and his undaunted courage, accom-
"panied by a zeal for the spiritual welfare of the sick and dying, made
"such a great impression on the minds of his congregation, that
"they ever after had unlimited confidence in him. Again, during
"the troubles of the abortive Insurrection of 1837-38, do we find
"Father Phelan the priest of order ; and there are living witnesses
"to-day to testify to the great influence which he exercised over the
"Catholic Irish in and around Montreal. Subsequently, during
"the disturbance which arose among the Irish on the Lachine
"Canal, we learn what control he had over their minds, for on that
"occasion his sudden appearance amongst them, with a few words
"from his lips, sufficed to quell that wild commotion, when passion
"had risen to its highest, whilst an armed force would then have
"proved but very ineffectual. "

"In his endeavors to promote the happiness of his congregation,
"he directed his attention towards the illicit liquor traffic, the bane
"of a community, and which renders the preacher's efforts abortive;
"and he succeeded to an extent which no other could probably
"have attained. His exertions in the cause of temperance are still
"proving fruitful, and will serve, perhaps, for many years to come,
"to perpetuate his memory. When he found matters ripe to glean
"the fruit, he established, in 1841, the St. Patrick's Total Absti-
"nence Society, which has worked so unostentatiously, and yet
"has accomplished so much good." The following year, 1842, a
change took place, which bore heavily on the Irish congregation
of St. Patrick. At the solicitation of Right Rev. Remigius Gattlin,
Bishop of Kingston, Father Phelan went to Upper Canada, and
became Parish Priest of Bytown (now Ottawa), after he had been
raised to the dignity of Vicar General. His removal caused much
sorrow amongst those to whose interest he had devoted so many years
of his life and labors, and there were many who could hardly reconcile
their minds to have him depart from amongst them. They, in their way
of judging, considered it a loss, and a loss which they imagined to
be irreparable ; yet God rewarded their respect and love for their

priest, by providing them with other saintly pastors of talent and energy. Previous to Father Phelan's departure, the Irish troops, whom he served, wished to acknowledge the debt of gratitude they owed him, so they presented him with an ornamented silver snuff-box, to mark how they appreciated his services.

The Irish Catholics of Montreal presented Father Phelan with an address, reciting his many works of Christian charity, and concluding as follows:

"Whithersoever you may be removed, our fervent prayers shall "ascend to the Most High for your temporal welfare and eternal "happiness; and we shall ever gratefully cherish the remembrance "of your piety, your fervor and your worth, with the most hallowed "feelings of our existence.

With hearts overflowing with gratitude, esteem, veneration, and "anguish, Reverend and Dear Sir, we most reluctantly say to you— "Farewell."

Peter Dunn,	Connell Gallagher,
Thomas Neagle,	Thomas McNaughton,
Andrew Conlan,	Daniel Mahony,
A. Doyle,	John Cassidy,
D. Cotterell,	Patrick Murphy,
Wm. Casey,	M. McDonnell,
James Warnock,	Francis Clark,
P. Muldoon,	Michael Purcil,
M. H. Darraugh,	John Warnock,
James Gleeson,	James Lahay,
J. P. Sexton,	P. Brennan,
Henry O'Donaughue,	Alex. McCambridge,
John Curran,	John McCann,
Charles Curran,	John Fitzpatrick,
John Maan,	P. Dromgoole,
Thos. Hewitt,	Matthew Ryan,
John Mahony,	Michael Kelly,
Daniel Murphy,	John Kelly,
Edward Murphy,	Michael Hyland,
John M. Tobin,	Christopher McCormick,
Francis Joseph Ryan,	Peter Henratty.

For further particulars regarding Bishop Phelan, the reader is referred to the little work above mentioned, where a full account is given of his great services to church and state as Bishop of Kingston.

REV. J. J. CONNOLLY.

FIRST PASTOR OF ST. PATRICK'S.

This zealous priest was the first pastor of St. Patrick's church. The following particulars of his career will be of interest. Rev. John Joseph Connolly was born in Ireland on the 8th of March, 1816, son of Michael Connolly and Mary Pendergast. He was educated at Montreal College, Seminary of St. Sulpice, where he was ordained priest on 1st June, 1844. For some time he taught English at the College, then joined the Seminary of St. Sulpice, and became pastor of St. Patrick's. His devotion and self-sacrifice during the ship fever were heroic. He established the " nine days' devotion " preparatory to the celebrating of the feast of St. Patrick, a religious exercise still in great favor at the St. Patrick's Church. He continued to exercise the ministry at that Church until 1860, when he resigned his connection with the Seminary and went to Boston, Mass., where he continued his zealous labors as a priest until 1863, when he died, aged 47 years, on the 16th of September.

Prior to the departure of Father Connolly, a meeting was held at St. Patrick's House, presided over by Edward Murphy, Esq., for the purpose of adopting an address to the reverend gentleman on his leaving the city for the scene of his future labors. A handsome sum was subscribed on the occasion, the spontaneous offering of the congregation. The rev. gentleman was deeply affected during the reading of the address, which was signed by Edward Murphy, as chairman, and Henry Kavanagh, as secretary, and to which he made the following reply :

GENTLEMEN :—

The address which you have just presented has affected me—affected me deeply. It makes allusion to scenes of a very distressing nature, and brings up many memories of the past. You will, I am sure, in the hurry of preparation for my immediate departure, excuse me from making a lengthened reply to your most flattering address. I cannot, however, permit the occasion to pass without assuring you that, however painful to the congregation may be the separation, it is not less painful to me, and that you judge correctly in supposing that nothing but a deep sense of duty could prevail on me to take a step productive of such pain to the congregation and myself. You say that I have labored long in your midst—even that

I have become prematurely grey in your service. You make allusion to the painful scenes of the yet too well remembered '47, and remind me that Almighty God has blessed my ministry. True, God has spared me to labor for a length of time amongst you ; true, that some of my labors in '47 were in the midst of disease and death, but in all trying circumstances the priest must be mindful of his duty ; he must feel the important embassy entrusted to his charge ; he must feel that he is the mediator between man and God, commissioned " to bind and to loose ; " that he must stand in the midst of danger, contagion and death to administer to the dying Christian his passport to the throne of God. Duty, strict duty, demands them from every anointed priest of God. If I passed through the trying ordeals of '47, '49 and '54, if I prepared for death and consigned to the silent grave for a period of six weeks or more some fifty adult persons per day, I was but doing what every priest would be bound to do under similar circumstances. I was discharging my sacred duty ; and if of all the clergymen who commenced at the beginning and labored to the end of that dire visitation, I was the only survivor, it makes me tremble, lest I alone should be found unworthy of the reward to which they were called in the midst of their labors.

In conclusion, I accept with feelings of deep emotion the address of Saint Patrick's congregation, and the accompanying substantial and unsolicited testimonial of their affectionate attachment ; and I beg to assure them that I feel deeply grateful for this unexpected proof of their kind feelings ; and though the call of duty removes me from their midst, it cannot remove from my heart the sweet remembrance of the past, and that as long as God shall spare me to celebrate the holy mysteries I shall not cease to offer my unworthy prayers for them on the altar of God.

(Signed)   J. J. CONNOLLY,

Priest.

FATHERS DOWD AND TOUPIN.

THEIR GOLDEN JUBILEE.

FIFTY YEARS IN THE SERVICE OF THE CHURCH.

Thursday, the 19th of May, 1887, was a gala day at St. Patrick's, Montreal. It will long be remembered by all who participated in the celebration of the golden jubilee of Fathers Dowd and Toupin. The enthusiasm was unbounded. The parishioners combining to do honor to them, nothing was left undone to add to 'he interest of the grand festivity. Nothing was missed that would add to the pleasure and happiness of the two worthy priests whom the congregation of St. Patrick's and the citizens of Montreal thus honored. Fathers Dowd and Toupin fully realized the generosity of their people in this respect. They were radiant with smiles, and few would realize from their vigorous appearance that they had passed fifty years of laborious work in the strict discipline of the Catholic Church. Their happy, healthy faces denoted that in all human probability they had in their separate capacities many years of useful work yet to perform in this, their chosen field of labor.

At Grand Mass an immense congregation was in attendance. The sanctuary was brilliantly decorated with flags, banners and bannerets, bearing appropriate mottoes and insignia, while the small altars and statues were beautifully decked with flowers of various hues, and lit up with lamps of many colors. On the Gospel side of the altar a throne was erected for the Archbishop of Montreal, and the clergy who assisted at the Mass occupied raised seats on either side of the sanctuary.

At ten o'clock precisely the church was filled, and as the altar-boys, seminarians, deacons, priests and prelates filed into the sanctuary, the scene presented was one of indescribable beauty. At the Mass, Rev. Father Dowd officiated, assisted by Rev. Fathers Varrley as deacon, and Kiernan as sub deacon. His Grace Archbishop Fabre had as assistant priest Rev. Father Marechal. The deacon of honor was Rev. Father J. Murphy, of London Diocese, Ont., and Sub Deacon of Honor, Rev. J. O'Rourke, of Odgensburg, N.Y. The following prelates and clergy occupied seats in the sanctuary during Mass: His Grace Archbishop Lynch, of Toronto; His Grace Archbishop Taché, of St. Boniface, Man. ; His Lordship Bishop Walsh, of London ; His Lordship Bishop Dowling, of Peterboro; Rev. Dean Murphy, of London, Ont; Rev. Dean Ramsay, of England, and Vicar General Rooney, of Toronto, with Rev. Fathers Geoffrion, Royer, O. M. I. ; Catulle, Conway, (Peterboro), Leclair, Godts, Verrau, Martin, Belanger, Brissette. Morin, McGary, Lonergan, McCarthy, Rouleau, Gaudin, Reed, Donnelly, O'Donnell, Bannon, (Chatham, N. B.), Duggan, Harty, (Hartford, Conn.), O'Sullivan (Burlington, Vt.), Laporte, Quesnel, Kiernan, O'Rourke (Port Henry, N. Y.), Gaudette, Deguire, Colin, Fahey, Rouxel, Barrette (Dakota), Corbett (St. Andrews, Ont.), and Lecompte, O. M. I., in addition to the clergy of the city of Montreal.

The choir of St. Patrick's was under the direction of Professor Fowler, and never was its musical ability displayed to better advantage. A new Mass, by Nini, of which Professor Fowler has the original manuscript, was sung for the first time in Canada by seventy-five voices with a full orchestral accompaniment. At the Offertory the orchestra played Wagner's bridal march with beautiful effect. The choruses were powerful and the solos were tastefully rendered by Messrs. J. Heenan, J. P. Hammill, J. Crompton, E. J. Casey and J. J. Rowan; Mr. William J. McCaffrey acted as leader.

THE SERMON

of the day was preached by His Lordship Bishop Walsh, of London, Ont. He selected as his text.

" Let the priests who rule well be esteemed worthy of double honor ; especially they who labor in the word and doctrine." 1s, Timothy, v. c., 17 v.

The Christian priesthood, dearly beloved brethren, is in the eyes of faith the greatest institution on earth of the power and goodness and mercy of our Lord and Saviour Jesus Christ. Through this priesthood the Son of God still continues to exercise here below the office of Redeemer and Saviour. It is His own eternal Priesthood working upon earth through human instrumentality, for the sanctification and salvation of immortal souls.

Our Lord is Himself the great High-Priest, and the Supreme Pastor of our souls. He was ordained by God the Father a priest for ever according to the order of Melchisedech. He once offered in a bloody manner on Mount Calvary the sacrifice of His body and blood, and that sacrifice fulfilled, summed up and completed all the bloody sacrifices of the old law. He was at once priest and victim. That sacrifice wiped out the handwriting of the decree that was against us, and purchased us with a great price. The victim was offered only on Calvary's hill, but the blood of the victim inundated the world, bringing salvation to mankind, and in principle washed away the guilt of all the ages. But our Blessed Lord was ordained a priest forever according to the order of Melchisedech. He will therefore institute a sacrifice answering to that of Melchisedech, a sacrifice which having the appearances of bread and wine, shall be the same as that of Calvary, that is, the sacrifice of his body and blood, offered up in an unbloody manner under the outward appearances of bread and wine, and this sacrifice he instituted when at his last supper he changed the bread and wine into his body and blood, and thereby instituted that clean oblation of the new law which in prophetic language was to be offered up for all time from the rising to the setting sun. Now as our Saviour was not to remain on earth for all time, but was soon to ascend into that heaven which he merited for us all, he ordained a priesthood which would carry out for ever the work of salvation which he in principle had accomplished, but which was to be continued in actuality on earth as long as human souls were to be saved.

It is of faith that at His last supper our Blessed Redeemer instituted the Christian priesthood when he authorized and empowered his apostles to do that which he had just done, namely, to offer up the holy sacrifice of His body and blood under the appearances of bread and wine. He then and there created the Christian priesthood, after having instituted the sacrifice it was ordained to offer for the glory of God and the salvation of men.

Jesus Christ, then, created an order of men whom He raised to a participation in his own eternal priesthood. St. Thomas says that ordination impresses a character, and that this character is a spiritual and indelible sign or seal by which the soul is marked for the exercise of the acts of the divine worship and for the teaching of the same to others.

And further, that priests partake of the priesthood of our divine Lord, the priesthood of Jesus Christ being the one only perpetual and universal priesthood ; all priests consecrated under the new law are made one with him, and share in His own priesthood. They are therefore empowered to offer up, on the altar, the tremendous sacrifice of the new law. They take bread and wine into their consecrated hands, and by the Almighty power of God, delegated to them, they change that bread and wine into the body and blood of Christ. At their bidding, Jesus Christ descends from his throne In heaven and becomes incarnate in their hands.

The sun stood still in the heavens at the command of Joshua ; but at the word of the priest, He who created the sun, and set it burning in the heavens, comes down from His divine throne to be offered up, an oblation of infinite value to His Eternal Father !

On the altar the priest stands as another Christ, and offers up to heaven the Son of God, immolated for the sins of His people. He thereby gives God infinite honor and glory. He deprecates and appeases his wrath, renders him propitious to sinners, and obtains pardon for the greatest sins, and unnumbered graces and blessings for souls. He is charged with the custody and guardianship of the body and blood of Christ. He keeps the key of the tabernacle. He carries our Lord whithersoever he wills. He, like St Joseph, is the guardian of our Lord on earth. He distributes this bread of life at the altar, to the rich and to the poor, the fervent and the tepid, sometimes, perhaps, to the unworthy. He bears him to the dying Christian, through crowded streets, through lonely and remote by-ways, through darkness and storm, into the cabins of the poor, as well as the homes of the affluent and wealthy. And what a guardianship is this! What a treasure is confided to the custody of the priest! It is the greatest trust that God could give to man; the most intimate and the closest relationship that could exist between the Creator and His creature, save that of the hypostatic union between God and man in Christ, or that of the divine maternity. Is it any wonder that the faithful can single out a priest, even though disguised, from among thousands, for they see on his face the reflex of the habitual presence of Jesus Christ and of his intimate companionship with him even as Moses bore upon his brow the reflected light of God from his converse with Him on the mountain.

The Christian priesthood is the instrument by which Christ continues the ministry of reconciliation and salvation upon the earth, by which he exercises the power of forgiving sins and the ministry of preaching and teaching, and of administering sacraments and all the details of sacerdotal duties.

Man, as an intelligent creature, has duties to fulfil toward God, has responsibilities to His eternal law. He owes to God the homage of his reason, the obedience of his will, the love of his heart.

Jesus Christ came to teach him his duties in · ese relations. Our divine Saviour came on earth, not only to redeem and save us by His sufferings and death, He came also to be our teacher and our guide, to reveal to mankind the truths of salvation and to unfold to their wondering gaze things hidden in the mind of God from all eternity. His mission was to unfold to man the whole plan of salvation what he should know and believe and do in order to be saved. He, therefore, spoke as no man had ever before spoken, and revealed to us the great saving truths of the Catholic religion that have ever since illuminated the whole firmament of time. The priest is the official guardian and teacher of these saving revelations of Christ. Our Blessed Saviour gave this sublime commission when immediately before His ascension He said to His Apostles: " All power is given to me in heaven and on earth. Going, therefore, teach ye all nations ; baptizing them in the name of the Father, and of the Son, and of the Holy Ghost, teaching them to observe all things whatsoever I have commanded you, and behold I am with you all days even to the consummation of the world." Mat. 28, 18. The people are bound under the pain of eternal loss to listen to and accept the teaching of the priesthood, for Christ says :

" Go preach the gospel to every creature. He that believeth and is baptized shall be saved, but he that believeth not shall be condemned." Mark xvi., 15, 16. And again : " He that will not hear the Church, let him be unto thee as the heathen and the publican." Matt xviii., 17.

The priest is Christ's ambassador and official representative to man " He that heareth you heareth me, and he that despiseth you despiseth me, and he that despiseth me despiseth him that sent me." Luke x, 16. The sacred word which the priest announces is not his own. It is the word of God, the word that enlighteneth every man who wishes for that light which is the light of the world. It is the salt and savor of the earth : the word that has changed the face of the earth and created a new civilization, that has enlightened the intellect, strengthened the will, and purified and etherealized the affections of the heart. The word that has come down through all the ages, pointing out to man his duty and responsibility to God, telling him of the vanity and emptiness of earthly things, reminding him of his immortal destiny and announcing to him the Evangel of divine mercy. This is the divine saving word which the Catholic priest is commissioned to proclaim in its purity and integrity to mankind. Members of sects may teach and preach, but they have no authority or mission from God to do so. They are not accredited ambassadors. They are but impostors, self-sent, or commissioned by those not having authority. They are like the false prophets of whom God complained when He said : " I have not sent them, yet they run, I have not spoken to them, yet they prophesy." Jeremiah xxiii, 21. " How shall they believe Him," asks the Apostle, " of whom they have not heard ? And how shall they hear without a preacher, and how shall they preach unless they be sent ?" Romans x, 14. Christ, himself was sent: " As the Father hath sent me, I also send you." John xx, 22. The ministers of the one true Church, the Church Catholic, and they alone, have the divine commission and authority to preach God's holy word.

But the priest is not only the herald and ambassador of Christ ;

he is also the minister of reconciliation, the dispenser of the sacred mysteries—the sacraments of our Saviour. Jesus Christ instituted in His Church the seven sacraments as so many channels through which the merits and graces of his sufferings and death were to flow, in life-giving streams for the salvation and sanctification of his people.

The Catholic priest is the accredited and authorized minister of these sacraments. He baptizes the infant, and makes it a child of God, heir of heaven and a member of the mystical body of Christ, which is His Church. In Confirmation, the Bishop, who has the plenitude of the priesthood, enrols the young Christian as a soldier of the cross, and imparts to him the grace and strength and courage to profess the truth openly, never to deny it by word or work, and to suffer and die for it if required. But one of the greatest and most awful powers, because it is God-like, which Christ conferred on the priesthood, is that of forgiving sins. This power is so essentially divine, so specially an attribute of the God-head, that when Christ said to the paralytic, "Go in peace, thy sins are forgiven," the multitude present, believing him to be a mere man, exclaimed : 'This man blasphemeth. Who can forgive sins but God alone ? " And in fact, when our Lord was about to confer this power, he made use of words and employed a ceremony which plainly indicated that He was about to perform a special and altogether singular exercise of omnipotence, infinite goodness and mercy, for He said to His Apostles, " As the Father hath sent me, I send you." He then breathed upon them and said : " Receive ye the Holy Ghost, whose sins you shall forgive, they are forgiven, them and whose sins you shall retain, they are retained." john, xx. 23.

St. John Chrysostom, commenting on this power conferred on the priest exclaims : "To the priest is given a power which God would not give either to the angels or archangels, for to these it was not said : 'Whatsoever you shall bind on earth shall be bound in heaven, and whatsoever you shall loose on earth, shall be loosed also in heaven.' Earthly princes," he continues, " have indeed the power of binding, but it is only for the body ; but the binding of the priest reaches even to the soul, and ascends to the heavens ; insomuch as what the priests do below, God ratifies above, and the master confirms the sentence of the servants."

The poor sinner weighed down with the burden of his sins, and the consciousness of his guilt, goes to the priest, and he, clothed with this God-power of forgiving sin, pronounces on him the sentence of absolution, and he that had been dead is come to life again. The lost is found; the prisoner is set free, and the prodigal is welcomed home again to the embraces of his Father.

Oh! what tears have been dried up by the merciful exercise of this power! What broken hearts have been healed, what troubled consciences have been quieted and set at peace and what blessed and immortal hopes have been enkindled in minds shrouded in the d rkness of despair! What death-beds have been robbed of their terrors, and made peaceful, blessed, hopeful and happy.

The Catholic priest is then, the minister and representative of Jesus Christ amongst men. In the language of the Fathers, he is another Jesus Chris., *Sacerdos alter Christus.* Like his divine Master, he goes about doing good, reclaiming the sinner, reconciling neighbors, bringing peace into families torn by dissension, instructing the ignorant, visiting the sick, comforting the afflicted, helping the poor, protecting the widow and the orphan; in a word, g ng glory to God in the highest, and bringing peace and happiness to men of good-will. The Catholic priest begins to care for man at the cradle, follows him with his ministry through all the phases and vicissitudes of life, and does not abandon him even when the last sod is put upon his grave. He follows him into the eternal world by his blessed ministrations, praying and offering sacrifice for his departed soul.

Faith, the sacraments, the sacrifice of the Mass, all the means o salvation left us by our merciful Redeemer depend, in the ordinary Providence of God, on the ministry of the priest, and cannot be given us without him. He is the central figure of the kingdom of grace established by Christ, the pillar of cloud by day, the pillar of fire by night, that is to protect us against all enemies, and guide us to the promised land.

There is no body of men known to history that have rendered mankind such great and inappreciable services as the Catholic priesthood. They redeemed the world from barbarism and conferred upon it the blessings of Christian civilization. They freed the slave and opened the doors of the dungeon to persons unjustly detained. They redeemed millions of captives from Mahometan prisons. In every centre of population they erected and supported hospitals for the sick and suffering, and homes for the poor and helpless. They invented a language for deaf mutes, and thus opened

up God's glorious creation with all its beauties, wonders and mean-
ings, and all the fountains of knowledge and the saving truths of
religion to minds hitherto imprisoned behind the adamantine walls
of unbroken silence and deafness, and shrouded in more than
Egyptian dark..ess. The great universities of the world that flamed
out like beacons on a dark and stormy sea, they founded and endowed.
Parish schools for children were established by them. To the
working classes they taught trades, as well as agriculture. They
taught the rich the duty of helping the poor, and they defended and
upheld human rights and liberties against the tyrant and oppressor.
The arts and sciences were brought to perfection by them. Printing,
sculpture, music, architecture, eloquence and poetry were, by them,
Christianized, perfected and immortalized. They have been the
greatest benefactors of mankind, the most virtuous, the most enlightened, the most disinterested, the most useful body of men that
ever lived. To say that some of them fell from their high estate
and lofty ideas, and were stained with sin and vice, is to admit that
they were human, and liable to the influences of human passions and
the seductions of the flesh ; but the fallen were the few; and the
great body, having on the panoply of God, led lives of purity, justice, and holiness, and by their great learning and splendid virtues
have made a track of light across the waste of centuries.

O, my brethren, let us respect, reverence and love the Catholic
priesthood. Let us be obedient to their teaching, and submissive
to their sacred authority. Let us inculcate on our children the
duty of respect and veneration towards them. Let us be indulgent
and charitable towards their failings, real or imaginary, for though
they are human, faults in them will look grave, which in other
men would be considered venial and of no account. Let us
protect and defend them against the talk of vindictiveness and the
shafts of calumny. Let us uphold them in their sublime but most
difficult mission, by our means, co-operation and influence. Let us
avail ourselves of their administrations and seek at their hands the
divine graces and helps confided to them, so that having followed
their guidance and made use of the means of salvation which it is
theirs to administer and enunciate we may one day reach and enjoy
that happiness for which we have been created and redeemed by
our most loving and most merciful God, to whom be honor, praise
and glory for ever and ever.

And, dearest brethren, if I have thought it pertinent to the occa-
c

sion that calls us together to dwell on the dignity and divine character of the Catholic priesthood, of its sublime duties and of the
incalculable benefits and immeasurable services it has conferred on
mankind, it is because we celebrate the Golden Jubilee of two venerable, devoted and holy priests who in fact and in public estimation
have during the long period of fifty years lived up to the ideal of the
Christian Priesthood; who have been priests according to the heart
of Christ; whose life has been a faithful pattern for the imitation of
their flock; who, like their Divine Master, went about doing good;
who were as another Christ amongst their people, feeding the hungry,
clothing the naked, sheltering friendless old age, protecting the
orphan, winning the hearts of children to Christ, forming by Christian
education the youth of both sexes on the eternal principles of Catholic
ruth and morality, breaking the Bread of Life to hungry souls,
preaching the Gospel of Christ to rich and poor alike, assisting like
angels of hope and comfort at the death bed, and by holy prayer and
sacraments preparing the immortal soul for the happiness and joys
of Heaven. For 39 long years Father Dowd has been doing the work
of Christ in your midst in this city. He landed here in 1848 to take
his part if required with the noble band of martyrs of charity who
sacrificed their lives in bringing the consolations and graces of religion to the dying Irish immigrants. Ah! who that witnessed them
can ever forget the heart-rending scenes that then took ace in
the fever sheds in the suburbs of this city; like a terrible nightmare
they haunt the memory for life. Those were indeed days that tried
men's souls—those were the days that tried the charity and zeal of
the priests and religious of this city as fire tries the gold. Hundreds,
nay thousands, of our countrymen, driven from their native land by
wicked laws and a dreadful famine, arrived on our hospitable shores;
but the famine fever, like an angel of destruction, pursued them
and smote them with pestilence and death. The fever sheds were
veritable Gethsemanes where hearts and souls were sorrowful unto
death; where hundreds of men and women were writhing in their
awful agonies. Father Dowd and other heroic priests entered that
Gethsemane like comforting angels to bring peace and hope to the
agonizing and to prepare their souls for immortal joys. Some of
those priests passed from their Gethsemane to their Calvary, where
they laid down their lives in sacrifice for their fellow men, but Father
Dowd was spared for other days and other duties and services. His
priestly virtues, his great talents and his sound judgment were so

conspicious as to attract the attention and to win the confidence and esteem not alone of the faithful but even of the Episcopate of Eastern and Western Canada, and in 1853 the Bishops unanimously petitioned the Holy See to appoint him Coadjutor Bishop of Toronto. The Bulls of his appointment arrived, but he resolutely declined the proffered honor and dignity, preferring to labor to the last amongst his faithful people. For twenty-seven long years he has labored as pastor amongst you, and God alone knows all the labors and sacrifices he has undergone for the promotion of the temporal and spiritual welfare of his flock. In season and out of season, in the cold of winter and summer's heat, in the midst of anxieties and trials, in absolute disinterestedness and in purity of purpose and loftiness of aim, has he invariably toiled to the duties of a true and faithful shepherd. St. Patrick's school, St. Bridget's refuge, St. Patrick's Orphan Asylum, are some of the monuments of his holy zeal. And in this connection may it not be said of him that "his bones when he has run his course and sleeps in blessings will have a tomb of orphans' tears wept on them."

Father Toupin has been for about twenty years laboring amongst the Irish Catholics of this great city. Seventeen years of his priestly life had been previously spent in the work of Christian education in Montreal College. It is impossible to estimate the merit of his work in this capacity. "What is greater," asks St. John Chrysostom, "than to train the mind and to form the character and mould the morals of youth! More excellent certainly than the greatest painter, than the most finished sculptor and than all others of this sort, do I esteem him who knows how to form the minds of youth and to mould them into shapes of beauty." How true are these words of the great saint and orator. For, when the greatest painting that ever lived by the breath of genius shall be covered with the mildew of neglect or destroyed by all-consuming time, and when the statues of an Apelles or a Michael Angelo shall have melted from marble into dust; the immortal mind, quickened into intellectual life by the wand of genius and moulded to virtue and holiness by the pious and holy priest, will live on forever a thing of immortal beauty and imperishable joy, a blessing to earth and a sister to the angels of heaven. You know better than I can tell you the qualities that characterize and enrich Father Toupin as a man and a priest. His heart is as tender as a child's. He is kind and charitable almost to excess, never refusing to render a service, no matter at

what inconvenience or sacrifice to himself. His hand is ever open
to relieve distress. In his community he is a model, in his public
ministry he is the holy and devoted priest, with him duty is supreme
—*salus animarum suprema lex*—night and day he has been ever
ready at the call of duty,—with him labor is a necessity and the
greatest fatigues in the service of his Divine Master are sweeter and
more welcome than refreshing springs to the traveller in the desert.
St. Augustine's motto is true of him " *Quando amatur non laboratur
aut si laboratur labor amatur.*" And so closely has he identified
himself with his Irish people, with their traditions, feelings and hopes
that he is literally "more Irish than the Irish themselves."

May these two devoted and holy priests be spared to labor yet
for many years amongst you, to give God honor and glory, to succour
and to save immortal souls, to enrich the Church by their virtues
and their merits and to exhibit in their honored lives the sublime
dignity, the exalted holiness and the Christ-like charity and self-
sacrifice that are the grand characteristics and the inalienable
properties of the royal priesthood of the Catholic Church.

THE BANQUET.

The Mass was then continued and immediately after it was
concluded, the Archbishops, Bishops and a number of Clergy,
including the Rev. Fathers Dowd and Toupin and the visitors,
proceeded to the Seminary of St. Sulpice at Notre Dame, where a
Grand Banquet was held. There was a large number of Priests
present and the Rev. gentlemen, Fathers Dowd and Toupin, were
heartily congratulated on the occasion of the fiftieth anniversary
of their ordination. His Grace Archbishop Taché, of St. Boniface,
who was, owing to a slight illness, unable to attend the ceremony
at St. Patrick's was present at the dinner. The party then returned
to St. Patrick's at 3 o'clock, and at 3.30 entered the Church, which
was crowded with the faithful of the parish and others, among
whom were noticed some of the most prominent citizens.

THE AFTERNOON MEETING.

AT the Morning Service the Rev. Father Quinlivan, who acted
master of ceremonies, announced that, in the afternoon at half
past three, a meeting would be held in the Church at which Fathers
Dowd and Toupin would receive the twelve congratulatory addresses
to be presented to them. The Blessed Sacrament was removed from
the Church and a platform was erected near the centre of the
aisle, from which the addresses were delivered. It was conse

quently more a secular than a religious service. Long before the hour appointed every seat in the Church was occupied; and among the congregation were noticed several leading Protestant citizens. The Hon. J. S. D. Thompson, minister of justice, accompanied by Mr. J. J. Curran, Q.C., M.P., and Mr. Edward Murphy, entered the Church about 3 o'clock, and were conducted to the seats of honor, immediately behind the platform. In front sat the Rev. Father Dowd and Rev. Father Toupin. Among those in the special chairs were Ald. Wilson, acting mayor, Ald. Grenier, Ald. Donovan, Ald. White, Ald. Laurent, Ald. Dubuc, Dr. Hingston, Rabbi Marks, Rabbi de Sola, Ald. P. Kennedy, Ald. Cunningham, Mr. Paradis, chief of police, Mr. Glackmeyer, city clerk, Mr. Owen McGarvey, Mr. Dennis Barry, president St. Patrick's Society, Mr. S. Davis and a number of other gentlemen. Prof. Fowler played a selection of airs on the organ, among which "St. Patrick's Day" and "Vive la Canadienne" were conspicuous, out of compliment to the nationality of the two clergymen who celebrated their golden jubilee. It is needless to say that the entire congregation of St. Patrick's Church was present. Father Quinlivan announced that decorum in the Church required that there should be no applause, and the order was religiously obeyed although occasionally, when the virtues of the two worthy fathers were extolled, there was a temptation for a demonstrative expression of love and veneration. The scene was not the less impressive because of its solemnity. Every seat in the Church was occupied, and there was uncomfortable standing room for the hundreds who thronged the aisles and passages. The honorary ushers of the occasion, Messrs. B. Tansey, Jas. J. Costigan, John Callaghan, P. Doyle, A. Brogan, J. H. Kelly, Jas. Tierney and Ed. Ryan, were active in finding seats for strangers.

At 3.30 Father Dowd and Father Toupin entered the Church from the Sacristy, followed by fifty clergymen. The Archbishops of Montreal and Toronto, and Bishops Walsh and Dowling bringing up the rear of the procession. The congregation rose from their seats as a token of respect when the two venerable gentlemen appeared.

Father Quinlivan then called on the

HON J. S. D. THOMPSON,

Minister of Justice, representing the Dominion Government, to pay his tribute of respect.

The Minister of Justice in his address said: By the kind arrangement which has been made this afternoon, it is my privilege to address the first words of congratulation to the venerable priests in whose honor this assemblage has taken place. As one connected with the administration of public affairs in this country, I esteem it a very great honor and a very great privilege to be able to congratulate Father Dowd and Father Toupin upon this glorious anniversary. I feel it an honor to be permitted thus to congratulate them, because in doing so I am doing honor to those whom Almighty God has already highly honored. They are here among you to-day endowed with the choicest gifts and the choicest blessings that heaven can bestow on them, and above all the two worthy Fathers have been granted the privilege 'o live to a time of life when they can see the reward of the fruition of many years of toil among the people of this great city. It is not to be wondered at that the people of Montreal have joined with the greatest unanimity in this celebration ; it is not to be wondered at that the people of this great parish of St. Patrick's rejoice to the core of their hearts at the occurrence of this jubilee. Since the ministry of those venerable priests commenced among you a generation has grown from childhood to manhood and womanhood. You have not only in all the vicissitudes of life experienced their kindly charity and their wise counsels, but it has been your good fortune to have seen and to have admired with others outside of Montreal those institutions which their charity and their zeal have founded in the community. My duty this afternoon is not merely to pay a personal tribute of humble respect to the two great priests whom we have met to honor. As one connected with the public affairs of the country, I am forcibly reminded that I am bound to do honor not only to the great priest, but to the great patriot as well. You in Montreal have been more familiarly acquainted with Father Dowd as a priest. Permit me to say, as one coming from a distant part of Canada, that we have known Father Dowd as a priest whose patriotism was too large for any one parish and too wide for any city. We have known him as a patriot, who, while holding the warmest love for his fatherland and the warmest love for the country in which he has spent so many long years, has never been afraid to speak his opinion on any public occasion demanding such expression—never afraid to speak the truth, and to speak it in trumpet 'tones which sounded from one end of the country to the other. I am, therefore, not only paying my tribute of respect to the illustrious priests this afternoon, but to the great patriots as well. On behalf of those from whom I have come, on behalf of the people of a distant portion of this Dominion, I have to say that it is our earnest hope that those venerable priests may be spared for many years of useful labor and successful work among you. It is my duty also to say here, as I expressed to Father Dowd this morning, and as I have been permitted to speak as one connected with the Federal Government, that I am charged with the message from the first Minister of the Dominion, that had his duties in Parliament permitted him he would have had great pleasure in coming here to honor his old friend—Father Dowd. I make those offerings of respect and congratulation, not as a politician, not as a man belonging to a party, but as a Catholic, and as a citizen to those deserving of all honor from those who love their religion and their country.

THE MUNICIPAL ADDRESSES.

TO REV. FATHER DOWD.

Ald. WILSON, acting mayor, read the following address on behalf of the City Council :—

REVEREND SIR,—It is with feelings of the utmost pleasure that we approach you to-day as bearers of a resolution unanimously passed by the Aldermen of Montreal, in council assembled, congratulating you on the fiftieth anniversary of your ordination to the priesthood, and in hearty appreciation of your long and faithful services to the cause of religion and morality. As the highest and most beneficent qualities of citizenship are involved in a pastorate such as yours, the City Council, speaking in the name of the Citizens of Montreal, without distinction of race, creed or class, could not let this opportunity elapse without paying a deserved tribute to the admirable manner in which you discharged these functions and the good that has flowed therefrom.

In the hope that you may long enjoy continuous health and strength to prosecute the ennobling work in which you are still engaged.

We remain, Rev. Sir,

Yours, etc.,

J. J. C. ABBOTT, Mayor,
ALD. WHITE,
ALD. STEVENSON,
ALD DONOVAN,
ALD. GRENIER,
(*As Committee*),
CHAS. GLACKMEYER,
City Clerk.

Mr. GLACKMEYER, City Clerk, read a similar address in French to Father Toupin which will be found on other page.

The following telegram was also read from the Mayor :—

OTTAWA, May 18, 1887.

Senate determines to sit Friday and Council will consequently sit to-morrow. With the greatest regret, therefore, I am obliged to forego the pleasure of presenting testimonial to the Rev. Fathers Dowd and Toupin. Pray present my felicitati⁓ ⌐ to them and express my extreme disappointment at being unable to attend.

J. J. C. ABBOTT.

THE CONGREGATION'S ADDRES ⸱.

Mr. EDWARD MURPHY read the following address from the congregation :—

REV. AND DEAR FATHER DOWD,—A half century ago you solemnly devoted yourself to the service of God, and were ordained a priest of His Holy Church.

The congregation of St. Patrick's Church of Montreal, for whom you have labored incessantly during four-fifths of that long period, approach you to-day with deep veneration and affection to offer you their sincere congratulation on your attainment of the fiftieth anniversary of your priesthood, and the accomplishment of fifty years of good, wise and noble deeds for the glory of God and the benefit of your people.

Forty years ago you entered the venerable and learned order of St. Sulpice—an order which has rendered such incalculable services to the cause of religion in Canada, and has given to the Irish of Montreal such devoted pastors as Fathers Richards, Phelan, Morgan, Connolly, O'Brien, Bently and Bakewell, and others who have died in their service, and an order to which they are still indebted for those who now labor so zealously in their behalf.

The daily and nightly performance of your duties as a priest, to which you devoted yourself with all the generous self denial of your holy order, making light of fatigue and hardship, cheerfully bearing trials, disregarding danger from contagion or exposure and combating obstacles in the way, have secured to you the confidence, esteem and affection of your people.

The visible monuments of your labors are numerous :—

The Orphan children of Irish parentage first received (in 1849) your parental care, and the St. Patrick's Orphan asylum, from a modest beginning, gradually assumed its present proportions, and its continued support has been the object of your constant solicitude.

The old and infirm were the next to receive your fostering care, and the inmates of St. Bridget's Home have daily invoked the blessing of God upon their kind and thoughtful protector.

The homeless by night were not left by you to wander and uncared for; and St. Bridget's Refuge for destitute poor has, for the past twenty-three years, opened its portals and afforded shelter and food to persons of all creeds and nationalities.

It was long felt that schools more in harmony with the wants of the people should be provided, and the St. Patrick's School for Girls, established by you, has fully met that requirement.

While providing ample accommodation for others, you neglected, too long neglected—your own comfort and that of your co-laborers. The parochial residence was totally inadequate to house you comfortably. At length you have been compelled to give attention to yourselves. The Presbytery, now being built, will afford you better—although still modest—accommodation.

When it was judged necessary to divide the old parish of Notre Dame into several, you, Reverend and dear Sir, ever watchful over the interests of your flock, obtained conditions which have smoothed the difficulties pertaining to that division.

Twice during your ministrations at St. Patrick's you have given unusual evidence not only of humility but of deep attachment to your people.

Your unaffected piety, ripe learning, mature judgment, great administrative ability and untiring zeal and devotion, long ago, marked you as qualified for the arduous and responsible function of Bishop; but the Coadjutorship of Toronto, to which His Holiness named you, had to be otherwise filled.

At a later period, designated for the bishopric of the diocese of Kingston, you again declined the dignity which would involve separation from your people.

To stimulate the ardor and zeal of your flock, you organized a pilgrimage to the centre of Catholicity, and to Lourdes, to which the eyes of the devout have for many years been turned.

It was accomplished, but not without misadventure; and the thoughts of those remaining behind were strained in your direction when the intelligence of possible disaster reached Canada. The citizens as a whole, and your own congregation especially, offered up prayers for your safe return, and when news of your safety came later, the joy expressed was general.

Who among your people has not had, on questions of difficulty, the advantage of your advice, and who has not recognized — though, perhaps, not at the moment—that the advice was in accordance with the unchangeable principles of right and justice.

Your wise counsel and guidance on questions for the general good have entitled you to public gratitude, and the Citizens of Montreal, by the mouth of their civic representatives, have embodied it in their address.

The maintenance of the institutions you have founded has, in great measure, ceased to give anxiety; the Church, however, in which you have so long officiated, and to which your congregation are so strongly attached, has been recently transferred to them— from tenants they have become proprietors—and the amount of the obligation incurred is large, and can only be met gradually. But your past wisdom, energy and devotion are a guarantee of future accomplishment, aided by that hearty co-operation on the part of the congregation which you have a right to expect.

Beloved Pastor, desirous of expressing in tangible form the respect, veneration and affection which they entertain for you, your congregation beg your acceptance of the accompanying purse, suscribed for the purpose of lessening the debt which you have assumed on the Church, trusting to use your own words, that " God will open new sources of revenue by inspiring many to remember the Church of their dear apostle when making their last will and preparing for eternity"; and they fervently hope that the Almighty may be pleased to prolong your life for the interest of religion and for the good of society.

On behalf of St. Patrick's congregation.

(Signed,)   EDWARD MURPHY, Chairman.

W. J. O'HARA, Secretary.

A HANDSOME OFFERING.

Mr. Murphy then presented to the Rev. Father Dowd a cheque for $17,206.21 as an offering from the congregation to pay off the debt on the Church.

TO FATHER TOUPIN.

Dr. HINGSTON then read the address of the congregation to Father Toupin. Dr. Hingston explained that it was intended to read the address in French, but at the request of the rev. gentleman himself he would read it in English.

TO THE REV. FATHER TOUPIN.

ᗡERMIT the Congregation of St. Patrick's to express to you their joy at your attaining the fiftieth year of Priesthood, and at the same time, their deep gratitude at your having devoted so large a portion of that period to their service.

It is now upwards of thirty-three years since you commenced your ministration amongst them; and the links of affection which those years of devotion on your part have thrown around them are irrefragable, and willingly bind them to you by the strongest and most enduring ties.

The sphere of your labors has, in some respects, been different from that of the Chief Pastor, whose Jubilee we celebrate to-day with your own. Yet your mission suffers nought by comparison. Like the Curé d'Ars, your functions have been those of the quiet, gentle, modest, retiring Priest, devoting himself with ever undisturbed affability, and with ever unalloyed kindliness of heart to the spiritual wants of the sick, and with a zeal which is rarely paralleled, and which it would be impossible to surpass.

Your work at St. Patrick's involved, almost of necessity, the partial sacrifice of your own beautiful language, in which you were admittedly a master. The members of the Congregation have always felt, and many times expressed, their appreciation of that generosity on your part.

Placed by fortune beyond the possibility of want or the necessity of labor, you have devoted all—all to the relief of the necessities of the poor and distressed—and, with such absence of ostentation that no one beyond the recipient, and often not even the recipient, could suspect whence came the generous relief.

But if you have been generous with your wealth you have been prodigal of what is more than wealth—ease, comfort, necessary rest. At all hours of the day you were ever at duty, or the possibility of duty. From baptismal font, receiving the new born into the Christian fold; to the sick, encouraging the sufferer, or smoothing the pillow of death.

Your alacrity, especially in responding to the night summons, has led to a suspicion in the minds of many, that, like a true soldier when in battle, you were ever ready, booted and helmeted for the

march. How many here can bear testimony that the night bell
was answered by Father Toupin in person, who, cap in hand, and
with a mysterious velvet bag under his arm, was prepared to accom-
pany the messenger whithersoever he would. Yet, notwithstanding
the frequent disturbance of sleep, no sign of impatience, no evidence
of irritation or annoyance was ever noticeable ; no word of reproof,
for being called' too early or too needlessly late was heard. The
summons to the confessional at hours the most inconvenient was
invariably quickly obeyed; and so long as penitent remained in its
vicinity, so long were you ready to listen, to admonish, to encourage, or to reprove.

Accept, *Soggarth Aroon*, their love for the love you have borne
them ; accept their gratitude for your labors in their behalf ; and
accept their fervent prayers for the prolongation of a life which has
been devoted exclusively to the service of God and to the spiritual
wants of His people.

TO REVEREND FATHER DOWD

REVERED AND HONORED FATHER,

ONTHS ago, playful fancy, ever ready to tell tales of the
future, began to paint us a picture. Earnestly we watched
its progress, eagerly waited for the last stroke when suddenly a brilliant glow bathed it in a flood of lightness. Your presence, Reverend
Father, has cast this roseate hue, and to-day our fancy's picture is
complete.

Need we ask your kind forbearance while to your respect and
esteem, we join our deep gratitude and filial love, to give honor to
whom honor is due.

Yes, dearly beloved Father, on this joyous day, that marks with
golden radiance fifty years of labor, devotedness and self-sacrifice,
we the least of your flock hasten to twine a chapelet of love and
reverence. Delicious dreamlike harmony has wafted our thanks in
entrancing strains ; each tiny rose bud has blushed our gratitude,
each floweret has breathed forth sweet fragrance in veneration of
the noble life offered at religious shrine. And yet what modesty !
what humility ! Who may sing the praise of a holy priest ? Angels,
methinks, must stand abashed as are recorded in the book of life the
souls saved by his prayers. His sacred hand holds the keys of
God's priceless treasures. He unlocks the portals and bids the
tender babe enter Christ's fold. He raises his hand, and at his sign

the dispairing sinner, crushed by the weight of guilt, is lifted up and
led on to God. A word whispered by a priest and in his hand is his
Creator. God's holy temple, which owes its beauty to his charity
and zeal, points to the home where are recompensed labor and devotion in God's cause. Such are the functions and work of an ordinary
priest. But has not your labor far surpassed all this ? The three
houses which surround the Church and are at present in such a flour-
ishing condition, do they not owe their origin, advancement and
success to your zealous and untiring efforts. The oldest of these,
which we inhabit, and which has given shelter to so many thousands
of children for the past (37) thirty-seven years is a standing proof
of your noble, generous and tender sentiments for the cause of poor
suffering humanity. Yes, you have indeed proved a father to the
orphan, a staff to the aged and a powerful support to Christian education.

These, O Reverend Father! are monuments which will perpetuate
your name in the realms of our Heavenly King, not such as prove
their worth by earthly measurement. Oh! no, the paltry bauble
ambition struggles to snatch from fame is worthless to you, who seek
your reward in God alone.

Our fervent prayer is that the remaining years of your precious
life may flow sweetly and peacefully ; may Angel hands remove the
stones that overlie life's pathway ; may the thornless roses ever
bloom, and may that Master whom you have served so loyally
bestow upon you the reward   the faithful servant. What glory
awaits you ! What a haven of rest will be yours within the folds of
the Sacred Heart where no more storms will threaten that bark you
guide so well, but where anchored safely you will celebrate an eternal Jubilee.

St. Patrick's Orphan Asylum.

TO THE REVEREND FATHER DOWD.

On the occasion of his Golden Jubilee.

Reverend and dear Father Dowd,

TO the many and eloquent tongues that have everywhere been
proclaiming your Golden Jubilee, the poor old people of St.
Bridget's Home beg leave to join their humble voices, and tell
you how proud we all feel on this grand occasion, which has been
the means of bringing to light your stirling worth and your well

deserved popularity among all classes and creeds of the City of Montreal. We may be the last to tell you so, but rest assured, Reverend Father, that we are not the least sincere in our expressions of love and admiration for one who has been everything to us, when houseless and friendless we were left alone in the cold streets of this large city to meet the sad fate that must have been ours, had it not been for the unbounded charity of your kind Irish heart.

Apart from your numerous and brilliant flock, the inmates of this noble Institution have ever considered themselves as belonging to your own private family. Others may glory in the fact of having you as a spiritual father, but to us alone has been given, in spite of our misfortune, the privilege of belonging to you, body and soul. When naked you have clothed us, when hungry you fed us, when homeless your fatherly hand raised this blessed roof over our heads. What more could you do ?

Yes, beloved Father, let us assure you on this solemn day, that your Orphan's Asylum, your St. Bridget's Home and Refuge shall form the three brightest gems in the crown which has been long ago prepared for you in heaven.

Such is the earnest wish and such shall ever be the daily prayer of
THE POOR OLD PEOPLE OF ST. BRIDGET'S HOME.

AU REVEREND JOSEPH TOUPIN, SS. DE L'EGLISE ST. PATRICE.

REVEREND MONSIEUR,

C'EST avec les sentiments d'un plaisir bien réel que nous venons aujourd'hui auprès de vous comme porteurs d'une résolution unanimement adoptée par les échevins de la Cité de Montréal en Conseil, vous offrant leur félicitations a l'occasion du cinquantième anniv-- aire de votre ordination comme prêtre, et le-r vive appreciations de vos services si longs et si fidèles dans la sainte cause de la Religion et de la Morale.

Les qualités les plus rares et les plus bienveillantes du citoyen se trouvant combinées dans l'exercise d'un ministère tel que le vôtre, le Conseil de la Cité se faisant l'organe de tous les citoyens de Montréal, sans distinction de race, de croyance ou de position, ne pouvait pas laisser passer cette occasion sans rendre un tribut bien mérité à la manière admirable dont vous avez rempli vos importantes functions, et à tout le bien qui en est découlé.

Avec l'espoir que bien longtemps encore, vous continuerez de jouir d'une santé robuste, et des forces qu'il vous faut dans la poursuite des travaux qui font partie du ministère que vous exercez.

Nous sommes, Révérend Monsieur,
Vos tout dévoués,

J. J. C. ABBOTT, Mayor,
J. GRENIER,
RICHARD WHITE,
P. DONOVAN,
A. A. STEVENSON,
Comité.
CHS. GLACKMEYER,
Greffier de la Cité.

Montréal, le 19 Mai 1887.

ST. PATRICK'S SOCIETY.

Mr. DENNIS BARRY then read the following address to Father Dowd from St. Patrick's Society :—

REVEREND AND DEAR FATHER DOWD,—The St. Patrick's Society of Montreal, of which you are the respected and beloved chaplain, desire to approach you on this, the fiftieth anniversary of your ordination to the priesthood, to join its voice with that of the other members of your flock in joyous felicitations on this happy occasion. The membership of St. Patrick's Society, embracing, as it does, Irish Catholics from all parts of the city and district of Montreal, entitles it to express the sentiments of all, including those who, though now priests, were fostering parents of that which Irishmen in this city and district feel justly so proud. You, as Parish Priest, have naturally been always in the van, and for the fruits of your ministry we have only to look around and see.

Dear Father, we beg you will accept the society's mite towards the general offering which is being made to you, knowing that your fatherly heart will understand the feelings of the members are not measured by the smallness of the amount; but that the many demands on the funds in the sacred cause of charity preclude them from making it commensurate with their desire and your worth.

In conclusion, the St. Patrick's Society prays that Almighty God may spare you for many years yet to watch over the interests of your congregation, and to witness the full fruition of your desires and aspirations for the well being and success of the many institutions which you founded for the education of youth and for the protection of the infirm, the orphan and the homeless.

On behalf of the St. Patrick's Society.

D. BARRY, *President.*
S. CROSS, *Secretary.*

THE ST. PATRICK'S SOCIETY TO THE REV. FATHER TOUPIN.

REV. AND DEAR FATHER TOUPIN,—The St. Patrick's Society of Montreal desires to join with the many who offer their congratulations to you this day on having attained the fiftieth anniversary of your wedding to Holy Mother Church and the service of the Sanctuary.

It would be superfluous to descant on the many sacrifices you have made in those long years of your ministry. They are known, and will be fondly remembered, by those to whom you have devoted your life ; for gratitude is the characteristic of the Irish heart, and the *Soggarth Aroon* is, if possible, more dear to them from the fact that he, in your person, has sundered the ties of kindred and race to labor for them in their hour of need.

To those greetings the Society adds a prayer : That those whom God has placed in your care may, for many years yet, have the benefit of that charity for them which is a part of your existence, your reward for which can only be fully known on that day when all secrets shall be revealed.

On behalf of the St. Patrick's Society,

D. BARRY, *President.*
S. CROSS, *Secretary.*

The St. Patrick's Society presented a cheque for $100.

THE TEMPERANCE SOCIETY.

Mr. Patrick Doyle read the following address from St. Patrick's T. A. & B. Society:—

REVEREND AND DEAR FATHER DOWD,—Amidst the general rejoicings on the occasion of your golden jubilee as a priest of the Church, permit your affectionate and grateful children of St. Patrick's Total Abstinence and Benefit Society to approach you with our feeble words of thanks and our humble testimonial of appreciation. Nearly forty of the fifty years of your priesthood have been devoted to the St. Patrick's congregation ; yet whilst laboring for the benefit of all, and thus enhancing so eminently the glory of the distinguished order of St. Sulpice, to which you have the privilege of belonging, you have found time to devote to the interest of the temperance cause in special connection with our society, of which you were once the revered and beloved president.

Your solicitude has ever been evinced in our behalf by the judicious selection you have invariably made of worthy and devoted clergymen for the position of our chief offic ., but in a marked degree you have given an impetus to our efficiency and a wider scope to our usefulness by a wise and comprehensive revision of our constitution and by-laws, enabling us to do good, not only as a temperance but as a benefit association, and placing both our branches on a firm and durable basis.

Out of your zeal and fo sight originated the constitution of the Irish Catholic Temperance Convention, embracing the various total abstinence organizations of the Irish parishes of Montreal and its vicinity, the extent and value of whose labors may be seen in the daily increasing strength of the principles we profess, whose adoption will ensure results so beneficial, morally and materially, to our people.

Under your paternal guidance, Divine Providence has deigned to bless our efforts, whilst comfort, as well as peace and harmony, have been made to reign in many a home through the adherence of our members to the rules of our association. We, as a body, without impairing our financial resources, are enabled to-day to request your acceptance of a small token of our grateful appreciation, in addition to the other gifts that are now being pressed upon you, and which, with that self sacrifice that has characterized your long, arduous and beneficient pastorate, you intend to apply, not to your own wants, but to the liquidation of the debt now weighing so heavily on this edifice, bearing the name of the apostle of Ireland—the glorious St. Patrick—where we hope our children, and their childrens' children may continue to worship, living, we trust, in the practice of the virtues of which your life has been so exalted an example.

God, in His goodness, has spared you, Reverend Sir, to see this happy day; not so long ago the hearts of your children were wrung in anguish when they witnessed you prostrated on a bed of sickness which threatened a lasting separation on this earth.

Now, thanks to Divine Providence, we behold you once more restored to health and vigor, and our earnest and constant prayer will be that you may long be spared, not only to our society, but to the congregation of St. Patrick's, the church of God and the advancement of the interests of our country.

Signed on behalf of the society,

EDWARD MURPHY, *President.*
P. DOYLE, *Vice-President,*
JAS J. COSTIGAN, *Secretary,*

The Temperance Society also presented a check to Father Dowd for $500.00.

OTHER ADDRESSES.

Father Quinlivan read the following address on behalf of the Ladies of Charity, signed by Mrs. Edward Murphy and Miss Emily H. Murphy. A check for $1,000 was handed in. Mrs. Murphy also presented two beautiful bouquets to the Rev. Father.

THE LADIES OF CHARITY.

Address of the Ladies of Charity of St. Patrick's Congregation, and their friends, to the Rev. Father Dowd, on the occasion of his Golden Jubilee Celebration :—

REVEREND AND BELOVED FATHER DOWD,—The Ladies of Charity of St. Patrick's Congregation, in their own name, and in the name of their friends, join your numerous children in congratulating you on this blessed and joyous occasion, the Sacerdotal Jubilee of your ordination, a glorious epoch, reached only by a privileged few.

The holy inspiration of providing a happy asylum for our little orphans, a comfortable home for our aged and infirm, has grown under your fatherly care and guidance beyond human expectations ; like the grain of mustard seed spoken of in the Gospel, " they have indeed multiplied a hundred fold. " The bazaars (38 in number), the principal support of these institutions, held yearly (with only one interruption) have had wonderful success, which is due, in no small measure, to the fostering care and heartwarm encouragement of our venerable and dear pastor. These bazaars, like many other good works, sprang from small beginnings ; we find in the records of the society that the first one took place in 1849, when the modest sum of $520 was realized,—the nett proceeds of the last, that of 1886, amounted to $4,740—forming up to the present the aggregate of $139,840.

May God grant you many long years to continue your good works, to watch over these institutions and to guide your loving flock.

The many fervent wishes breathed for you to-day, dear pastor, ascending, like incense, to the throne of the Most High, form, as it were, a chain, the links of which are composed of the prayers, the grateful tears and sighs of the widows and orphans and many others in affliction whom you have comforted and strengthened by kind words and wise counsels.

The sweet words, "Soggarth Aroon," have ever been dear to the Irish heart, but never with more reason than when we look back, through the long vista of years, and think of the life of self-sacrifice and untiring zeal manifested towards us by you, our devoted Parish Priest. In conclusion, allow us to to thank you for the fatherly interest you have always taken in the works of the Ladies of Charity, and accept this offering towards your last great undertaking, the liquidation of the debt of St. Patrick's Church.

MARIA G. MURPHY, *President,*
EMILY MURPHY, *Secretary.*

Montreal, May 19th, 1887.

Father James Callaghan read the address from the Confraternity of the Living Rosary.

CONFRATERNITY OF THE HOLY ROSARY.

We, the members of the Confraternity of the Most Holy Rosary of the blessed Virgin, rejoice on this day. It recalls to our minds the epoch of the introduction of this salutary devotion into our English-speaking Catholic congregation more than forty years ago through your pious instrumentality. For that length of time you have watched over the interests of our Sodality with a fervor which the fatigue of your ministry or the multiplicity of your enterprises of charity could neither relax nor diminish. You were our first director and you have always held out to us a protecting hand. The thousands of familiar instructions which you delivered with such paternal unction had a telling effect, and many a broken hearted sinner returned to the sweet embraces of God's friendship through the fervent and eloquent appeals which you addressed to Our Lady of the Rosary. When within the last few years Pope Leo the Thirteenth called upon His children to storm Heaven with the powerful weapon of the " Hail Mary," in the recitation of the Beads, your energetic and decisive co-operation admitted of no bounds. Your xhortations ceased only when all your flock, young and old, rich and poor, lettered and unlettered, joined their voices in one common and general invocation to Mary Immaculate. The month of October, each year, is one of intense consolation in our parish. The thirty-one days are spent within the precincts of our church in honoring, by special evening exercises, the Queen of the Most Holy Rosary. Often times we have been encouraged, in giving our small monthly fees, to hear you say, with a smile of delight, that our little contributions though individually insignificant in appearance, have collectively bequeathed in great part to the St. Patrick s Church the vestments and sacred vessels used in the celebration of the most august sacrifice of the Mass.

Frequently you have spoken to us about the importance of being faithful to the devotion and meetings of the Sodality to which we belong.

Nothing inspires you with a more sensible and palpable love of the rosary than the progress which the Holy Catholic Church is making in the scale of human aggrandizement. Some would fain attribute the increasing preponderance of Leo the XIII. to a kind of ungovernable fatality, or to the natural course of events, without any special concurrence of supernatural agencies ; but your piety, founded upon your affection for Our Lady of the Rosary and upon the marvellous results obtained in the days of St. Dominic and in other trying times of the Church's history, discovers in the pleasing and agreeable form of prayer of the Rosary the secret explanation of this strange phenomenon.

Thanks, then, reverend and dear Father, for your kindness in our regard, and receive, if you please, this token of our appreciation of your eminent qualities.

SODALITY OF THE ROSARY.

Father Martin Callaghan read the address from the Children of Mary.

THE CHILDREN OF MARY.

REV. AND DEAR FATHER:—At last it has arrived, the long-expected and long-wished-forday. We, the children of Mary, gather around your venerable person and hasten to lay at your feet the homage of our sincerest congratulations and the threefold tribute of our reverence, gratitude and devoted affections.

Since the establishment of our association, twenty-three years ago, you, our Reverend Father and deeply cherished friend, have ever

been our guiding star, guarding and safely directing our frail bark
on the perilous sea of life. The viscissitudes incidental to time have
severed and scattered our members far and near. Many have been
harvested into the celestial granary and are, let us hope, enjoying
the reward of their good works ; others have yielded to the attrac-
tions of divine grace and anchored in the harbor of the religious
state, where peace and security reign with undisputed sway. Anx-
iously did we anticipate this day, and most earnestly did we sup-
plicate the Throne of Mercy when, during your pilgrimage to the
Chair of Peter, and during your protracted illness, the phantom of
doubt kept us hovering between hope and fear. But our prayers
pierced the clouds, and the ever faithful Sogarth, whose locks have
been silvered, and whose steps have grown feeble whilst toiling in
the vineyard of Our Lord seems to regain something of his former
strength and buoyancy of spirits, as he lends an ear to the festive
lays which his loving children are rehearsing on all sides upon this
day of days, which it is granted only to the privileged few to
behold. Ah, yes, favored children of St. Patrick! well may you
sing your joyous song. Make these walls reverberate with
strains of your most enchanting melodies. Let the tones of the
organ break in the most soul-stirring appeals ; still in our midst
is our father, our pastor and our friend. Half a century ago, on a
bright and glorious May morning, when nature was arrayed in its
loveliest garb and all creation seemed aglow with beauty, he vowed
an everlasting farewell to the world with all its prospects, with all
its riches, pleasures and honors, and in his dear native land, in the
island sanctified by the prayers and tears of St. Patrick, he pledged
himself solemnly to follow closely in the footsteps of the Divine
Master. Did he regret his engagemer s ? No, never ; annually he
renews his clerical promises at the fc of the altar on the feast of
the Presentation of the Blessed Virgin, and with what rapturous
delight must not the angels of heaven have listened as they heard
him repeat once more, in this his golden jubilee festival. "The Lord
is the portion of my inheritance and of my cup ; it is Thou that
wilt restore my inheritance to me." But why seek in language
to find utterance for the sentiments which overflow our hearts ?
Must we deprive silence of its golden eloquence ? But one word
more—one fervent prayer. Reverend and dearly beloved Father:
You have a great and all-absorbing wish at heart ; may you be
spared to see this realized, and then, O Blessed Mother of God,

thou whose devout client he has ever been, into whose care
and tender solicitude he has so often commended his dear and
grateful children, from thy starry throne gaze upon him, guide his
footsteps, till, safe in the haven of eternal rest, thou shall deck his
brow with the laurels of victory.

Master McKenna then read the address from the Children of the
Catechism. At the conclusion of the address the most interesting
scene of the jubilee was witnessed. A number of little girls, beau·
tifully dressed, approached Father Dowd and presented him with
$500 in gold. Each child held a silver plate on which were the
gold pieces.

CHILDREN OF THE CATECHISM.

REVEREND FATHER,—I have come to represent and to speak in
the name of all the boys and girls who attend the Sunday Catechism of this parish. It would indeed look strange if we let this
occasion pass by unnoticed—if we were to be left in the shade and
doomed to remain silent. We readily acknowledge that we are not
perfection, and may prove at times a trifle troublesome, but still we
claim to be your children, and should avail ourselves of this opportunity publicly to express the manifold sentiments with which we
have been always animated in your regard, and which we realize
more vividly upon this thrice blessed day. Once you saw the days
through which we are passing. Education was vested with charms
which you could not resist and did not fail to appreciate. Thanks
to the most favorable of home influences, religion experienced no
difficulty in stamping upon your youthful mind and heart an impress
luminous, distinct, profound and indelible. You grew in the knowledge of supernatural truth, and rapidly advanced in every Christian
virtue. Your standard became the Divine will. You have always
cherished and followed it. God called you to the super-eminent
dignity of the priesthood. You responded to His call, and already
fifty years have elapsed since, crossing the threshold of the
Sanctuary, you dedicated to His service all your faculties, energies
and resources. With the inspired Psalmist did you exclaim in all
the fervor of a heaven-born enthusiasm: "How lovely are thy
tabernacles, O Lord of hosts. I have chosen to be an object in
the house of my God. For better is one day in Thy courts above
thousands." We congratulate you upon all the glory which, through
your instrumentality, has accrued to the Most High ; upon all the

inestimable graces with which you have enriched the various flocks
committed to your charge; upon all the beautifully diversified forms
which your piety has assumed; upon all the humility, charity and
zeal which you have accomplished; upon your sterling worth,
unimpeachable integrity, and unswerving allegiance to principle;
upon the almost unrivalled reputation which you have won for
yourself by excelling in all that is true, just, honorable, noble
and magnanimous. For more than a decade of years you were
engaged in catechizing the little ones of our parish. You knew
how to descend to their level, and esteemed yourself regularly
happy in their midst. You solidly instructed them in the tenets
of our holy faith, trained them in the practical love of duty,
and inspired them with veneration for the Sacraments. You dug
deep and wide the foundations upon which the superstructure of
happiness, both temporal and eternal, should rest. We owe you a
special debt of gratitude. You furnish us with striking evidences
of the interest which you take in our cathechetical instruction.
You may justly pride in the magnificent results obtained through
the doctrinal system of St. Charles Borromee, which you introduced
into the city, and frequently do you advocate our cause in the
pulpit. You provide us with a band of teachers eminently qualified
by their intellectual culture and disinterested zeal for the important
task which they voluntarily impose upon themselves. You spare
nothing to encourage us, and annually you preside at the distribution
of our premiums. We promise not to be ungrateful for the many
precious favors which we have received at your hands. In what-
ever circumstances we may be placed, we will comply with all our
obligations as Christians and Catholics. We will always cling to
the teachings of our infallible Church, and to the traditions of the
dear old land where you spent the earlier portion of your life, and
where the spirit of St. Patrick still prevails in all its beauty, strength
and splendor. We have been plying a variety of ingenious industries, and succeeded in gathering the sum of no less than half a
thousand dollars. We are delighted to have it in our power to make
you a golden offering, and the only thing we feel like regretting is
that alchemists have not yet discovered the philosopher's stone,
which we would greatly like to have a little while in our hands, so as
to cancel the whole of the debt weighing upon our dear old St.
Patrick's Church. Please accept our gift from children who
represent all the different sections of our Catechism.

Catholic Young Men's Society.

Rev. and Dear Father,—In the midst of this vast concourse of happy hearts, none ought to rejoice more than the members of the Catholic Young Men's Society of Montreal. The very pleasing duty of gratitude, apart from the higher and more exalted sense of justice and equity, has awakened in us a thrill of grateful emotion. You are indeed, Reverend Father, the founder of our Association. We owe our social existence to your creative genius. Twenty years ago the pious zeal which you had on all previous occasions displayed in the performance of good works suggested to your mind a new field of useful labor. The institution and organization of our society, and its consolidation upon the basis of wise and prudent constitutions, are the precious relics of your intellectual industry in our behalf. Year after year your love and affection for the male Catholic youth of our young and prosperous city grew more and more intense, and ke; : on inventing new and attractive forms of innocent amusement and recreation so indispensable, particularly at our period of life. Your long tried experience and deep observation of character had signalled out to your keen and watchful eye the dangerous and delusive snares held out to an inexperienced youth. Accordingly you have embodied in our rules the very essence of the important lessons which the glorious past had taught you. Your far-seeing providence saw, likewise, the avenues of material prosperity open out in brilliant colors before the gaze of Catholic youth. Without a moment of delay, you established on a firm and solid footing those literary conferences that have contributed so powerfully to bring into bold prominence the many sterling qualities which, till then, had remained dormant and silent in the solitude of their beings. If, to-day, so many young men of Catholic parents fill positions of trust and responsibility in our midst, they owe their elevation and promotion to your indefatigable efforts in procuring them the means of progressing in everything advantageous and profitable. To encourage the members in the carrying out of their thoroughly religious mission, you accepted the directorship, which you held for years and which you transmitted afterwards to a succession of priests of your excellent order, who, by their learning and piety, have continued and are now continuing to follow up to the work so nobly and so generously inaugurated by your marvelous activity.

Your admirable spirit of self-sacrifice has been largely shared by the army of presidents and other officers and members, whose countless numbers are now scattered over the broad continent of America, and whose true and genuine principles acquired in youth are still their beacon light in the vicissitudes of life and a forcible argument of persuasiveness for their fellow-citizens.

To foster and develop the empire of religion amongst us, you approached the Chair of Peter and humbly craved the spiritual intervention of the immortal Pius IX. That august Pontiff hearkened to your pressing entreaties, and lavished with an unsparing hand his indulgences upon our association, whose principles and tendencies you advocated with all the earnestness of an apostle of youth.

In a word, you have neglected no resources whereby you might realize the words of the illustrious Leo XIII, in his eminent encyclical letter, dated the 20th April, 1884. He writes : "That the objects of our desires may be the more easily obtained, we once more urgently commend to your fidelity and watchfulness the care of youth, as t' : hope of human society. To its formation give your greatest care "

Receive, therefore, Rev. and dear Father, the expression of our sincere gratitude, and please accept as a tribute of our unalterable d· otedness this small gift wnich we joyfully present to our exceedingly kind benefactor and loving father.

CATHOLIC YOUNG MEN'S SOCIETY OF MONTREAL.

THE LEO CLUB'S ADDRESS.

We, the last-born of your spiritual children, have come forward on this solemn occasion to reiterate the profound sentiments of loyalty and affection so universally and so spontaneously voiced by the senior associations.

We lawfully pride in being called your Benjamin, and we flatter ourselves with the throught that we do enjoy an unusually larg: share in the big heart of our affectionate parent.

Your love for us, dear Father, does not fall upon a barren and sterile ground. No. It has brought into play the echo of sweet gratitude. " Excelsior " is our motto, whether we are praised or censured. If, at times, the playfulness of our age has betrayed us into some little freaks of what we thought a peculiarly funny nature, your justly merited reprimand always came in time to season the exuberance of our joy.

We appreciate your corrections, always given with gentleness and firmness. To say the least, they have made us none the worse. We even presume to say that we are on the advance line.

We do not forget the lessons of wisdom which you have ever inculcated to us. You have taught us particularly to love our holy religion. We have followed your inspirations. We have selected for our chieftain and leader the immortal Leo the Thirteenth. Under his guidance and direction we are sure to be on the right side, and were we to become like him we would be far from being pitied.

Our rich and gorgeous banner is a standing memorial of our attachment to the successor of Peter.

To knit together the various elements which enter into the composition of our Leo Club, we glory in being the bodyguard of the sacred Tabernacle where resides in glorified though hidden splendor the Holy of Holies. Each successive month since our organization in 1884 has witnessed in our parochial church a heavenly sight. We have vied with one another in our zeal to approach the Holy Communion. Union, strength and mutual happiness have been the recompense of our close union with the Most Sacred Heart of Jesus.

Our young minds have not been left in the shade. Our mission here below is to shine by the brightness of our intellects as by the purity and innocence of our lives. Our literary academy has always given you intense pleasure.

Perhaps, dear Father, we are talking too much about ourselves and not enough about our kind Father, whom we cannot speak enough about.

You will therefore pardon us, but bear in mind, dear Father, that when the heart is overflowing with joy, as on this day, there is a necessity of speaking even at the cost of being a little tiresome.

Please accept, dear Father, our little offering, and believe us,

Ever yours,

LEO CLUB.

ADDRESS OF ST. PATRICK'S CHOIR.

REV. AND RESPECTED FATHER,—The members of the choir of St. Patrick's church beg to express their gratitude at being permitted the opportunity of tendering to you and to your very worthy coadjutor, the Rev. Father Toupin, their sentiments of the most profound veneration and esteem upon this joyful occasion. It has always been our ambition to contribute in our humble way to the impressive rendering of the Divine service in the church, and if our efforts in this regard have been in any degree successful we may confidently attribute it to the unceasing interest you have always manifested in our progress, and the kind and generous encouragement you have ever seen fit to bestow upon us. In a similar manner we have to acknowledge many kind favors at the hands of Rev. Father Toupin, and we earnestly pray that an all-wise Providence may graciously extend your days to continue the great and noble work of charity and education which you have so successfully inaugurated and promoted since your connection with the parish of St. Patrick.

As a slight tribute of our gratefulness, and as the result of our efforts on behalf of the celebration of your Jubilee, we beg your acceptance of the accompanying, being the proceeds of the entertainment given in the Queen's Hall on last Tuesday evening, and which was rendered doubly enjoyable by the presence of yourself and of Rev. Father Toupin.

Very respectfully,

THE MEMBERS OF ST. PATRICK'S CHOIR.

Mr. Riardon, on behalf of St. Mary's Congregation, also read an address.

FROM THE PROTESTANT COMMUNITY.

Mr. M. P. Ryan then read the following address :—

REV. AND DEAR FATHER DOWD,

A most gratifying part in the happy proceedings of this joyous and memorable occasion has been assigned to me to offer you, and your estimable and indefatigable colleague, Father Toupin, on behalf of a large number of your fellow-citizens, clergy and laity, who are not members of your communion, their cordial congratulations on your attainment of your Sacerdotal jubilee.

So rare and signal a favor of Divine Providence conferred upon the congregation of St. Patrick's Church, as the celebration, at the same time, in the same parish, of the fiftieth anniversary of the ordination of two priests whose life-long services in this community have given such general edification, has been rejoiced in by all your fellow-citizens without distinction of race or creed.

In proof of this general feeling, I have the great honor of presenting to you this tangible testimonial, the spontaneous and voluntary expression of the respect and esteem of those citizens who so gratefully appreciate your long, distinguished and successful labors in the cause of religion, charity, unity and peace.

M. P. RYAN, *Treasurer.*

The address was accompanied by a cheque for $600.

Rev. Father Toupin then ascended the pulpit, and expressed his thanks to those who had so highly honored him, and remarked that many of the eulogies bestowed upon him were entirely undeserved. He would leave the task of thanking the various societies to his more eloquent co-worker, Father Dowd.

REVEREND FATHER DOWD'S THANKS.

The Reverend Pastor of St. Patrick's Church then delivered his reply. Addressing Hon. Mr. Thompson, he said :

HONORABLE SIR,—I need not say that the presence of the Minister of Justice, bringing assurances of good will from the Federal Government, is, on this occasion, an honor I appreciate in the highest degree. The puny efforts I may have made, from time to time, to protect and to promote harmony amongst our varied population, did not, certainly, merit such distinguished approbation. Permit me, however, to say it—this public approval of even my humble efforts in the interests of peace does you honor. It shows that your Government is based upon the principles of peace, and, consequently, upon the principle of impartial justice to all, without which there cannot be possible either peace or harmony amongst the people of this country. Do not believe, honorable sir, that your Government is in the least my debtor. What I did was done in the interests of society, and from a conviction of duty alone. My conduct would not be different under any other Government. I know nothing of party divisions, nor of party struggles. I am, in fact, a blan in politics. But I earnestly desire, and even pray, that the interests of our dear young Dominion may be always entrusted to the care and guidance of men of ability and good will. My illness of last year brought me under heavy personal obligations. Your honored chief was constant in his enquiries. You, honorable sir, and others of your colleagues, came to my sick room. To duly appreciate this kindness one must be seriously sick, as I was. This duty of comforting the sick is too sacred for politics to meddle with it. It is a duty of pure friendship, and of thoughtful and disinterested charity.

Accept my heartfelt and lasting thanks for your honored chief, for yourself, and for your honorable colleagues. May God bless you and give you long life to labor for the good of your country.

TO THE CITY COUNCIL.

The honor of this presentation was not expected by me. I could not hope that a body so representative and so important as the Corporation of Montreal would notice our little family feast in so extremely kind and complimentary a manner. My not deserving this distinction does not, I assure you, make me less grateful. One thing gives me real pleasure ; in your indulgent appreciation of the little good I may have done for Montreal in my position, I have a guarantee of the forgiveness by my fellow-citizens of my many short-comings. I will add with sincerity that I value this compliment the more because it comes from men I particularly esteem. The late flood, a time of public suffering, has shown them to be, not only cool and calculating men of business, but has proved them to be worthy of their position, men of charity, of tenderness of heart, and of self-sacrifice. Mr. Mayor and gentlemen, I thank you for your friendly wishes. Be assured of my gratitude, and of my affectionate remembrance of your great kindness. Father Toupin cordially adopts these sentiments as his own.

TO THE CONGREGATION.

GENTLEMEN OF THE COMMITTEE, REPESENTING ST. PATRICK'S CONGREGATION.

GENTLEMEN :

IT is not in my power to find suitable words to express my thanks for the great kindness of your beautiful address. Warm friendship diminishes the faults of a friend, just in proportion as it magnifies the least good he does. This is exactly what your friendship has been doing for me. All my faults have disappeared, and the little good I have done has grown into such proportions that I must look at it twice before I can recognize it as my own. Fifty years ago such kindness would likely have been dangerous to me. The "old boy" would no doubt whisper into my ear something like this:—If you were not somebody, if, in fact, you were not a great man, these friends, so serious and so enlightened, could not say such things of you. Fifty years ago this would have been a real danger; to-day, if I know myself, it is not so. Behind, and not far behind, the opinion which your affection and your kindness form of my actions, I see the judgment of another tribunal. Before long, I cannot say how soon, I shall have to stand before that tribunal, and answer to an all-seeing, and all-knowing God, for the thoughts, words and deeds of my fifty years of priesthood. You, my dear friends, will not be there to excuse me. I shall be there all alone with my works, by which I must stand or fall for eternity. Poor silly vanity has not much standing room here. You speak of the institutions of charity and of education that have come into existence during my time in St. Patrick's. Yes, institutions that now prosper, under the blessing of God, have been founded, and are doing good work in the cause of the poor and of religion. The St. Patrick's Asylum, our orphan's home ; the St. Bridget's refuge, the home of our old and helpless poor, and the night shelter of the homeless stranger; and St. Patrick's school, the pet nursery of our little girls ;—these stand around St. Patrick's Church as so many outposts to complete and to guard the work of religion. Yes, my dear friends, you may indeed thank God for selecting you as instruments to do His work, and for giving you a docile spirit to obey the impulse of that charity with which He filled your hearts. It is through you that God is a father to our fatherless little orphans ; it is through you His loving providence provides for all the wants of our old, and feeble, and helpless poor. Will not God bless you for thus using a generous portion of the means He gave in doing His own work ? I do with all my heart congratulate you, for in thus doing your duty you secure a great reward for yourself, and you leave a bright example to those who will come after you. But you seem to think that I have had a principal part in the good that has been done. This, my dear friends, is a mistake. Give me a cool shade from which I may look on ; and do you take the burden and the heats of the day ; then our positions will be about correct. When there was question of our different enterprises I had of necessity to lead and to suggest ; this was a necessity of my position as your pastor. But is it not a pleasant thing to lead when a multitude of willing hands follow you? When, in fact, you are followed by many willing to take you up upon their own shoulders, and to carry you on faster when you commence to lag? This was my happy position as your pastor. I led you by just one little pace in advance of the multitude that pressed on from behind. Were I to delay or become indolent I would have to bear the shame of your zeal and energy, and besides I would have my heels tripped up without mercy. The suggestions I had to make were always received in a good spirit, and when examined and matured by your practical wisdom and experience they were always promptly carried out. You stopped at no sacrifice of time or money to complete the work once begun, and to secure for it a prosperous future. You now commence to enjoy the fruits of your sacrifices. God has evidently blessed the institutions you raised to His honor, and for the relief of His suffering members. They are in full work, owing no debt, and consequently are no longer objects of over-anxious solicitude. But what am I to say of your offering of to-day, intended to diminish the debt of St. Patrick's Church? When the project of taking hold of this enormous debt ($124,000) was first sprung upon St. Patrick's congregation, I was staggered and I lost all my courage. I at once asked my Superior to place this unexpected charge in younger hands. I felt that the responsibility of such a debt would soon crush me into the grave. My Superior would not listen to me, so I had to remain in harness, and to do my work the best I could.

It is with a certain amount of confusion that I now make this confession. Long as I lived in your midst, and worked with you, I did not thoroughly know you—there were depths in your charity which I had never sounded. It required my old age, my very feebleness, and the decline of my faculties, to bring out fully the resources of your charity, of your love for your holy religion, and of your goodness of heart. The hundredfold and life everlasting shall certainly be yours, for you make God Himself your debtor. What you give out of your substance to His house God will accept as given to Himself, and He will reward you accordingly. You allude to my services on the occasion of the division of the old Parish of Notre Dame. As this matter can now be approached without any undue feeling of any kind, I will state the simple truth. I gave such advice as I believed to be in harmony with the laws of our holy church. This I did as a simple duty, being your pastor. You followed my advice in the spirit of true Catholics. The Holy Father spoke, all obeyed, and ever since we are happy and content. As you have put on this ground I ask you to do an act of justice, late though it be. You sent two delegates to Rome to explain your case to the immortal and loving Pius IX. Their action had, probably, a determining influence on our question. The delegates undertook the labor and the hardships of that long journey at their own sole expense, and yet they never received a word of public thanks. I venture to thank them to-day in your name. One of them is dead, poor D'Arcy McGee, we will pray for his soul. The other is yet spared to us, so I shall name him—the Hon. Thomas Ryan. On an occasion like the present I may be pardoned if I go back a little in the history of our people in Montreal. A few facts on the testimony of an official, if not an eye-witness, may be usefully put on record. When I came to Montreal in 1848, the Irish Catholic population numbered about 12,000 souls, and amongst them there were only a few proprietors, say half a dozen, more or less. Now we may put down the number of our people at 30,000, and the proprietors by hundreds. When in 1849 I undertook to build the St. Patrick's Orphan Asylum, I gathered contributions from the Irish Catholics of the whole city, who gave me cheerfully according to their means ; only three gave me $20 each. Now, in order to reduce the debt of St. Patrick's church, five heads of families living in St. Patrick's parish contributed $5,000—$1,000 each. Let us go back a little further. When in 1848 I arrived in Montreal, I met an Irish Catholic, who, when a boy, attended the first Sunday services of the Irish Catholics, conducted by a priest of the Seminary, the Ven. Father Richards. This man attended mass and religious instruction in the dear old Bonsecours church in 1817. The congregation was small, though it contained all the Irish Catholics residing in the city. A few years earlier it was not known that there were any Irish Catholics in Montreal. Most probably the fact of their existence became known to Father Richards by his being called to attend a dying Irish Catholic. The kind father enquired of the messenger if there were other Irish Catholics in Montreal? On being answered in the affirmative, he said : Send word to them all to meet me in the Bonsecours church, at a time he named. When, at the appointed time, the good father came to the church he found there exactly thirty persons. He conducted them into the sacristy, where he gave them advice and instruction ; and sent them home with a promise that they should have, from that time forward, a regular religious service. Commencing with a familiar instruction given in a sacristy to thirty individuals, the religious service of the Irish Catholics has never since been interrupted, and to-day is performed in five churches of the city, with solemnity, to 30,000 individuals. The little grain of mustard seed is grown into a large tree. The thirty unknown exiles in a strange land have multiplied into a population of 30,000 citizens, having their own place in society ;

provided with churches for their religious wants, with happy homes for their children, and with prosperous institutions for the care of their orphans and helpless poor. Do you not discover in all this the watchful Providence and the loving care of God in our regard? They who have gone before us were not ungrateful; their good conduct proved their gratitude—so shall ours.

The solemnity of this occasion reminds me of a serious duty. I have to ask your pardon for all my shortcomings during the thirty-nine years I have labored amongst you. Your great charity would fain cover them all; but, my friends, it is this great charity of yours which makes me see them more distinctly and feel them more keenly. Did you love me less, I would, perhaps, grieve less for the faults I have committed against you. I can say it with truth, that I always sought your good, but how often, whilst administering fraternal correction, as duty required, was the tender sweetness of charity wanting; so that, in trying to remove perhaps a lesser evil, I caused a greater one by inflicting pain and suffering. So many proofs of your kind confidence satisfy me that you will forgive me; but even that will not satisfy me fully—ask of God to forgive me also.

What I have said is addressed alike to all the St. Patrick's congregation, yet I must admit that certain portions of it, certain societies, having made special efforts for the success of the feast, deserve separate mention. We will first take up the St. Patrick's Society. Its privileges place it first amongst our societies; its duty imposes the necessity of giving good example when the interests of St. Patrick's are in question. I beg to thank the St. Patrick's Society for its extremely kind mention of the small services I may have rendered the congregation, and I congratulate it on its generous assumption of the responsibilities of its honorable position. We will take the St. Patrick's Temperance Society next. They will please accept my hearty thanks for their over-kind and heartful address, richly supplemented by their generous offerings. I owed them much already for the services they are always willing to render. My debt is now largely increased; so that I believe I shall die without paying them. May God bless them, and make them always examples of virtue in St Patrick's parish. The ladies of St. Patrick's congregation put into the treasury of the church a large amount. To the sums already given by their husbands, these good ladies add the money intended for their own use, and this they again increase by their labor and by

E

every artifice of charity. Their good works are done for God in secret: I shall not profane them by holding them up to human praise. The Confraternity of the Living Rosary join cheerfully in the united effort to reduce the debt of the church. Already remarked for their punctual attendance at their regular devotions, the members of the Living Rosary become to-day examples of generous devotedness by their abundant offering to the house of God. May God bless and reward them. The children of Mary are never behind in any good work. They are always generous, always open-handed and kind. To give back freely to God a portion of what they received from Him is to them really a work of love. They are convinced that it is for their advantage to keep God always their debtor. The zealous Director of the Catechism is evidently bringing up his dear children in the way they should go. Their first lesson in charity has been nobly given to-day in favor of dear St. Patrick's. To help the common fund, candies, fruits, tops and balls are all forgotten. The cents are banked, and made to produce large interests by means of concerts and other industries, and all to reduce the debt of St. Patrick's. To-day the children of the Catechism may well be proposed as an example to be imitated by persons who learned their Catechism long, long ago, but who have perhaps forgotten a little of its practical teachings. God will bless those dear children, and will bless their parents for their sake. How am I to thank the St. Patrick's Choir for the rich aid they have procured for St. Patrick's Church. This aid is indeed valuable, because of its amount, and because of the labor, study, and talent expended to procure it. Others have given their money, the St. Patrick's Choir have given their money also; but with it they gave the sweat of their brow, and the prolonged anxiety of their minds. God will bless them. If they sought a merely temporal reward they would find it in their great success, and the increased reputation of the choir. The Catholic Young Men's Society, too, have given proof of their good will. These excellent young men, in addition to the example they give of the practice of other Christian virtues, and of a laudable desire for their intellectual culture and improvement, give to-day a beautiful example of charity to the young men of their age. May God help them to persevere in the paths of virtue.

The Leo Club must not be forgotten. They, too, have put their hand to the good work. I love the Leo boys—full of fun, of noise, and of piety. They say that the Leo boys are wild ; that may be so, but in the meantime I am sure they are quite in earnest about their duty. They will play tricks when they can, but they will not neglect their prayers nor their monthly confession. Full of heart, full of daring courage, they are also full of Irish faith. All in all they are the very materials I would select for the future of St. Patrick's parish. Besides my own immediate flock, other dear friends have shown their goodness. In my poverty I can make but one return, and I make it to all. I earnestly beg of God to bless them and their families, and to reward them according to the richness of His own bounty. There is scarcely a yard in the city I did not visit, at one time or another, in the exercise of my ministry. My visits are no longer the same, but my heart is not changed ; it has a place for all the people as before. Hence I shall not name St. Ann's nor St. Mary's, nor St. Gabriel's, nor the other more recent divisions. I shall name none in particular ; I have but one heart, and they are all there. In this happy concert of peace I would wish to avoid even the appearance of making a distinction. I have to do so, however, as a matter of justice. It is not now for the first time that Protestants have proved to me that there is a common ground of holy charity, upon which all Christians can meet and shake hands, and be kind to one another. During many long years when we were poor, and our little orphans were numerous, more than half the proceeds of the yearly bazaar for their support came from the open-handed charity of our Protestant friends. Need I allude to the warm-hearted sympathy that was received from the same quarter on the occasion of our pilgrimage to Rome? Can I forget these things? And remembering them, can I allow this solemn occasion to pass without recording a grateful mention of them, and without expressing my most cordial and sincere thanks. You remind me that I have been a peacemaker. I admit it ; throughout my life I have done my best to inculcate the ways of peace. For this I deserve no thanks. As a priest I am of necessity a minister of peace. Besides, the experience of my long life has shown me that the fruits of peace are sweet and full of happiness, whilst the fruits of discord and contention are bitter and conduct to misery and to death. I desire to see peace reign in every place, but I desire specially to see it reign supreme in our dear old City of Montreal, where I have labored the greater part of my life, and where, ere long, I hope to repose in peace. Once more I thank you all in the fulness of my heart. May God bless you for your charitable indulgence to His poor old priest and may He reward you a hundred-fold for your great goodness and liberality. I can say no more.

The proceedings in the church then ended.

Solemn benediction of the Blessed Sacrament was given in the evening.

CONCERT OF ST. PATRICK'S CHOIR.

The Queen's Hall was packed to its utmost capacity, with an audience composed of all classes and creeds, the occasion being the inauguration of the series of entertainments which are to mark the golden weddings of Rev. Fathers Dowd and Toupin. the esteemed priests of St. Patrick's Church. Shortly before 8 o'clock the two venerable clergymen, accompanied by the rev. gentlemen of St. Patrick's, entered the Hall and took their seats in the private box, which had been specially reserved for them. The programme, which had been specially prepared, opened with the Grand March from "Tannhauser," by the orchestra, which was well received. The members of St. Patrick's choir followed with a chorus from the "Lily of Killarney," which displayed careful preparation ; in fact, all the numbers in which they participated showed the different parts to be very evenly balanced, and reflected great credit upon the choir master, under whose direction the entertainment had been organized. The chorus, "Birds of Spring," was particularly pleasing, as in addition to the full choir and orchestra, some twenty-five young lady amateurs took part, giving to this number an effect which cannot be reached by male voices alone. Mrs. Page-Thrower's solo, "Deh Vieni Non Tardar," was rendered in that lady's well known artistic style. Miss Alice Crompton, in her selection from "Il Barbieri," showed to excellent advantage her possession of a cultured voice, and a degree of taste and expression, which was the subject of universal admiration. In response to a rapturous recall, Miss Crompton gave "Killarney" in a manner which fairly carried away the house. Miss Alice Seymour, being prevented by her severe cold from giving her number, Mr. Robert Lloyd kindly filled her place, and sang "The Harp that Once Through Tara's Halls" with such effect, that he, too, had to respond to an encore. Miss Jessie Grant's piano solo, "Belisario," elicited warm applause. The Toreador song from "Carmen" was excellently rendered by Mr. John P. Hamill, who possesses a fine baritone voice. Mr. Ralph Bolton's rendition of " Kathleen Mavourneen " was one of the gems of the evening, as was also his " Believe Me, if all those Endearing Young Charms," with which he responded to a recall. A tenor solo from Mr. J. Heenan from " Aida, " and a quartette, "The Youth's Warning," by Mrs. Page-Thrower, Miss Alice Crompton, Mr. Ralph Bolton and Mr. E. F. Casey ; a march from " Lohengrin " by the orchestra, and the chorus "God Save Our Native Land " by the choir, completed the musical portion of the programme, which was under the skillful *baton* of Prof. J. A. Fowler, organist of St. Patrick's choir, who is entitled to great credit for the excellent manner in which the affair was carried out.

The programme was diversified by an address from Mr. W. J. O'Hara, in the course of which he said :—The choir of St. Patrick's have conferred upon me the privilege of announcing on their behalf the object of this musical festival, of conveying to you their cordial welcome, and expressing their gratification at the generous way in which you have responded to their invitation to initiate this evening the festivities in honor of the golden jubilee of our venerable and beloved pastor, Father Dowd, and his devoted and estimable and, shall I say, indefatigable coadjutor, Father Toupin. It is not for us, ladies and gentlemen, to anticipate the words of cordial congratulation, of grateful acknowledgment, of eloquent, affectionate and truthful encomium, which will, doubtless, emanate from the overflowing hearts of a numerous people on next Thursday afternoon ; nor need I refer here to the tangible form in which their respect, gratitude and affection will shape themselves, beyond wishing that the form may be of the largest and most plethoric size, and withal graceful, symmetrical, and harmonius. It is a great pleasure for the choir to find themselves in such complete accord, not only with the congregation of St. Patrick's, but with the citizens of Montreal generally, and the whole Canadian people, who have shown their delight to honor these great and good men who have so well served the noble and holy cause of religion, charity and peace. Much as I would wish to do so, I must refrain from expatiating upon the visible and enduring monuments of Father Dowd's long and eminent services for the love of God and his people—his priestly devotion ; his care of the poor ; the provisions he made for the orphan, the aged and infirm, the hungry and homeless, the

destitute and houseless by night; his efforts to provide proper
education for girls; his constant anxiety for the comfort and welfare
of others, and his neglect of himself; the protecting arm he always
had uplifted to wisely and firmly guard his flock from every evil;
his sacrifices of episcopal dignities out of humbleness of spirit, and
a desire to remain with the people of his first spiritual love, among
whom he saw his mission—his provident and energetic efforts to
maintain the institutions he founded; the pilgrimage he made to
Rome and Lourdes to promote the spiritual zeal of his people; the
danger encountered, the anxiety felt by all, the fervent prayers for
his safety, and the general joy at his return—all these things are so
well worthy of dutiful recognition and remembrance that they will,
doubtless, enlist the silver tongue of eloquence on Thursday next.
The poem in honor of Father Dowd, written for the occasion by
Miss Anna T. Sadlier the gifted daughter of his life-long friend, the
distinguished Irish-Canadian lady literateur, Mrs. Sadlier, will now
be recited by Mr. P. McCaffrey.

Mr. McCaffrey then ascended the nostrum, and in a style which
gave evidence of talent and cultivation, recited the following beautiful poem :—

FIFTY YEARS IN THE MASTER'S VINEYARD.

How beautiful upon the mountains are the feet of him that bringeth good tidings and
that preacheth peace ; of him that sheweth forth good, that preacheth salvation —
Isaias lii., 7.

'Twas morning and 'twas May, the air was sweet
With bloom, upon an Irish shore, its green
Proclaimed the Resurrection, fragrant buds
Spake of a beauty that no eye hath seen.
When at the altar step, a youthful form,
With upraised face, with heart and soul a-glow,
Craving the sacerdotal grace, the while
He heard the whisper falling soft and low :—
Beautiful upon the mountains are the feet
Of him that brings good tidings, preaches peace.

A priest forever ! and the youth goes forth,
Goes to the vineyards as the morning breaks
Over the hills—to " lift the watchman's voice. "
" To preach salvation, " manhood's prime o'ertakes
Him toiling in the field, with words of peace,
Planting the works of mercy, reaping souls,
Bearing true witnesses in the name of Christ ;
While loud and long the echo upwards rolls :—
Beautiful upon the mountains are the feet
Of him that brings good tidings, preaches peace.

Time marks its way in silver on his head,
His step grows feebler and his voice less strong.—
And sounding near him is the mighty song,
A people's honor and a city's praise ;
His footsteps still unswervingly pursue
The path of faithful ministry, he hears—
For, singing it pass on the fruitful years :—
The hymn that charmed the youth of long ago,—
Beautiful upon the mountains are the feet
Of him that brings good tidings, preaches peace.

And monuments arise upon his way,—
A temple hung with memories more rare
Than Eastern marbles, or than gems of price,—
Whence aged men have passed away with prayer,—
Where youthful ones have grown to mellow age
Where boys have swiftly reached to men's estate,—
Each generation sounding as it goes
The anthem of his praise, O blessed fate !
Beautiful upon the mountains are the feet
Of him that brings good tidings, preaches peace.

Those homes wherein the old go down life's slope
In prayerful calm,—wherein the orphans bless
This more than father's care and tenderness,—
Where homeless ones find shelter in the night.
These words cry out 'mid countless silent deeds,
'Mid schools, 'mid charities, his praise who stood
With gaze upon the everlasting hills,—
Still swells the song " for him that shows forth good !"
Beautiful upon the mountains are the feet
Of him that brings good tidings, preaches peace.

The church's humble son, most fearlessly
He cries while pointing out the shiny way,
" The light which Patrick lit at Peter's torch
Alone can guide us to eternal day."
He loves the grand traditions of his race,
For Faith has lent them its divinest grace ;
But—patriot of Heaven—he hears above
All earthly sounds, the canticle of love—
Blessed upon the mountains are the feet
Of him that brings good tidings, preaches peace.

      *   *   *   *   *   *   *   *

'Tis May again —the voice of spring is heard
Far from green Erin's shore in Ville Marie,—
The fifty years' rich crown of honor won,
The visions of the youth surpassed, O see !
His jubilee—true priest of God !
The people press—take up the golden hymn,
Which, when new years have won him added crowns,
Shall greet him from the choirs of cherubim ;—
" Blessed upon the mountains are the feet
Of him that brings good tidings, preaches peace ! "

CELEBRATION AT ST. PATRICK'S SCHOOL.

ONE of the most interesting features in connection with the celebration of the Golden Jubilee of Revs. Fathers Dowd and Toupin, and one which will long be remembered by those who had the pleasure of being present, was the entertainment given by the pupils of St. Patrick's School, on Wednesday afternoon, the 18th of May. The hall was tastefully decorated with evergreens and banners bearing appropriate mottoes. As Fathers Dowd and Toupin entered, accompanied by their Lordships Bishop Walsh, of London ; Bishop Dowling, of Peterboro ; Rev. Fathers Conway (of Peterboro), Duggan, Harty (Hartford, Conn.), Quinlivan, James Callaghan, Bro. Arnold, and a number of lay gentlemen, ten of the young ladies executed an instrumental duet, entitled "Golden Strains," on five grand pianos, with a violin accompaniment, the latter being furnished by Rev. Martin Callaghan. As the last notes died away, one of the junior pupils stepped forward and presented a floral tribute to the distinguished prelates, who had honored their festival with their presence. Then followed the "Jubilee Commemorative Poem" (composed for the occasion by Mr. W. O. Farmer), and which was read in an admirable manner by Miss Frances Donahoe. The Angel Visitants, Patricia, Josepha, and Maria, then claimed the attention of the audience, and quite charmed their hearers. The Fairies with their Gifts and Song here made their appearance, having danced across the seas to do honor to the Golden Wedding of their beloved Father ; they brought with them a bouquet of wild flowers gathered from around his childhood's home, and also a blackthorn from the banks of the river Dee, which they presented, and were duly appreciated by Father Dowd. The next on the programme was " Le Tresor de nos Cœurs, " by fifteen of the smaller children. This was followed by a French address read by

Miss Mary Monette, and a presentation to Father Toupin. The
"Good old Days," recalled by former pupils, was heartily acknow-
ledged by the Rev. Fathers. They were represented by the Misses
R. and M. McNally, Lillian Morgan and Katie McCall. The
following address was read by Miss Rose McNally, in a style which
betrayed no ordinary degree of elocutionary skill:

THE PINCH OF SNUFF IN THE GOOD OLD DAYS.

The programme is almost over of music, of song, of play ;
The notes of solo and chorus have floated fore'er away,
We've listened, but all in vain for a sound or a word of praise
Awarded to our dear school-time. Oh, they were the good old days !
So, feeling that we've been slighted, a gentle protest I bring,
And crave but a moment's hearing, while of those old days I sing.
'Twas then that we worked and studied, at play, too, we had our share ;
A smile from our loving pastor would banish our every care.
These cares more heavy at times, if, scanty the sheaf we'd reap
" Philosopher" we were called, and the word had a meaning deep.
So deep that we never dared to boast of our title new,
That title's extinct ,I'm told) or now held by a very few.
But oh, there were joyful days that we know we shall long recall ;
Days marked by a special record for great as well as for small,
Our marks had been all perfection, therefore we were good enough
To get from our dear Father no less than a pinch of snuff.
Oh precious that pinch to us ! A diploma of merit rare
Could hardly be higher prized, brought home with more tender care.
'Twas tied in the kerchief's corner, or placed between leaves of book.
While other less fortunate ones upon it would sadly look.
So, for sake of the good old days, we have brought you a pinch of snuff.
Of the joy it so oft has caused us, we never could say enough.
And we are sure no medical friend your taking it will prevent,
'Tis your old time " witches " and " fairies" that it to you have sent.
And with it we have brought a gift, from the friends of those good old days.
Of the days we recall so often with sweetest of unsung lays—
As you've earned the right to rest there's a talisman in this chair,
Just as soon as you're seated in it will vanish all anxious care.

The pinch of snuff was contained in a very pretty floral box, and
assumed the form of $100 in gold. Miss May Curran read to
Father Dowd an address which concluded with a wish that all
present would be privileged to celebrate his Diamond Wedding.
Every countenance reflected the sincerity and earnestness of the
wish. The address was accompanied with the presentation of a
magnificent gold Chalice, entwined in flowers, and containing $300
from the present pupils of the school.

In replying, the Rev. Father said that he had often spoken to
them on different things; sometimes on their studies, on their
sewing, knitting, and domestic economy in general, as he was quite
experienced in those various branches, but to-day he had to treat a
subject which he thought was a very indifferent one, himself. When
he was a young priest, just beginning his ministry, fifty years was a
long time to look forward to, but now that it had passed it seemed
to have slipped through his fingers, and he had done very little
during that time. He asked the children to pray for him that his
future years might be spent in doing good among the people with
whom he had spent such a long period of his life. He then thanked
them for the generosity they had shown in trying to aid him to pay
off the debt of the church. He could prove his gratitude only in
praying for them that they would always continue true to their
faith, and worthy children of their holy patron. In conclusion
Father Dowd bestowed his blessing upon all present, which example
was followed by their Lordships.

Then followed the reading of the following jubilee commemorative poem by Miss Frances Donohue. This poem was written by
W. O. Farmer, and speaks for itself.

JUBILEE COMMEMORATIVE POEM.

Since time began hath mankind, right or wrong,
Been proud to lionize in tale and song,
The transient triumphs of ambitious men,—
To laud your heroes of the sword or pen—
Your Nelsons and Napoleons, men whose names,
Great tho' they be, proclaim but wordly aims!
Your men of state of Bismark's subtle school—
By fair or foul means, men who'd ruin or rule.

But if such men as these must challenge praise,
In blood and pillage, men who pass their days,—
How much more worthy they of our applause,
Who seek to be the heroes of a cause,
Such as on Calvary's Mount forever broke
Pagendom's pow'r and Satan's sinful joke!
A cause that hath regenerated man,
His faults redeemed and all but crushed the ban
That Adam's "fall" bequeath'd to all his race,
When forth from Eden driven in disgrace!

Such, cherish'd Father, is the cause that thou
Hast from thy earliest years espoused till now !
A vet'ran in its sacred service grown—
A champion, thou 'midst all its champions known.
For half a century hast thou baffled sin,
Confounded vice and virtue taught to win—
From pitfalls leading manhood's steps aside.
At once our earthly and our ghostly guide !
" Peace and good will " thy glory 'tis to preach
To all thy flock—to close up every breach
That in their ranks from time to time is made
By scandal's evil tongue or passion's aid.
Nor are the " little ones " o'erlooked by thee,
As all assembled here to-day may see,
Thou hast provided means the best to suit
" To teach the young ideas how to shoot,"—
Abodes of learning cared by teachers blest
With all those parts that best adorn the breast !

But, though a Christian in the strictest sense—
Tho' sturdiest in the old, old Faith's defense,
Ne'er hast thou, surely, been a bigot deemed,
All sects esteeming, by all sects esteemed !
Whilst in thy breast hath glowed a patriot's zeal,
Subdued but strong for mother country's weal !
And why, pray, doubt but that still in thy day
Our aspirations for old Ireland may
Accomplished be, and Home Rule's flag be seen
Floating in triumph over College Green !

Thrice welcome, then, thrice welcome cry we all
This happy day—one long, long to recall !
This gala day, our first, best golden feast—
Thy fiftieth anniversary a priest !
Long may thy days be spared—thy years prolonged,
To right the Church's wrongs, so often wronged !
By precept and example still to show
The duty that to God and man we owe !
And thou, true scion ! of a gallant land—
Of *la belle France!* whose brave sons, hand in hand,
With Erin's oft have marched in days gone bye.
At duty's call prepared to do or die—
" God and the right " united still to shield
Where dangers threatened most by flood or field ;
We greet thee too ! to thee, too, we extend
Our loving sympathy, thou well-tried friend !

With our lov'd Pastor hast thou toiled for years,
Partaker of his joys and hopes and fears !
In thee faith and good works at once combine
To make the perfect Christian and divine,
Whilst in the veins of none blood warmer runs
Than that which courses thine for Erin's sons !
God-speed thee, then ! and may thy future be
One long uninterrupted Jubilee !

The remainder of the programme was as follows :
Cantata, "We strike the Harp with Glee." Polylogue, "The Golden Day."

Part 1st. Introductory.

Part 2nd. "Angel Visitants," The Fairies with their Gifts and Song. Instrumental solo, "Whispers from Erin." Violin and pianos, "The Golden Day."

Part 3rd. "A Rosary of Years" Vocal Quintette, "A Prayer for Our Father." Polylogue, "Le Tresor de nos Cœurs."

Instrumental music, "Les Noces d'Or." The "Good Old Days," recalled by former pupils. Grand chorus, "And doth not a meeting like this make amends."

Final, instrumental music.

BIOGRAPHY.

THE REV. PATRICK DOWD,

PASTOR OF ST. PATRICK'S CHURCH OF MONTREAL

*F*ATHER DOWD, as his parishioners love to call him, was born in the County Louth, Ireland, in 1813, of respectable parents in good circumstances ; at an early age he evinced an ardent desire to devote himself to the church, he made his classical course at Newry. He went to Paris in 1832, when he made his theological studies in the Irish College in that city ; his course was a brilliant one. In 1837, May 20th, he was ordained Priest by Monseigneur Quelen, Archbishop of Paris ; after his ordination, he returned to Ireland where he lived about ten years, six with the Archbishop of Armagh, and was President of the Diocesan Seminary of that town for one year.

In 1847 he resolved on joining the order of St. Sulpice, and went to Paris for that purpose, after spending a year in their *noviciate* he was admitted a member of that illustrious body. He came to

Montreal, 21st June, 1848, and officiated at St. Patrick's Church, when Father Connolly left St. Patrick's, in 1860, over 27 years ago, Father Dowd was appointed, by the Superior, Director of the congregation, a position which he has retained ever since.

Shortly after his arrival he saw the necessity of an asylum for Irish orphans here, and early in 1849 established one, and the same year commenced the building of the present St. Patrick's Orphan Asylum, which was opened in November, 1851.

In 1865 he established St. Bridget's Home for the old and infirm, and the Night Refuge for the destitute. In 1866— he erected the present commodious building on Lagauchetière street for the Home and Refuge.

One can hardly estimate the vast amount of suffering relieved, and of the good done by these charities.

In 1872 he established St. Patrick's School on St. Alexander street, opposite the Church,—the building is large and commodious, this school is for girls, and is conducted by the Rev. Ladies of the Congregation of Notre Dame, whose reputation as educators is known all over America. Over 500 pupils attend this school. This splendid institution is another monument of Father Dowd's untiring zeal to forward the interests of his people.

Aided by the Ladies of St. Patrick's Congregation, he organized the Annual Bazars for the support of the Orphan Asylum,—these Bazars have been from the first remarkably successful; the first was held in October, 1849; they have been continued yearly till this date,—the last held was the 35th *Consecutive Bazaar*, and we have pleasure in recording that Protestants as well as Catholics assisted in this good work.

Besides the above Father Dowd has done much to ornament and beautify the interior of St. Patrick's Church, which next to Notre Dame is the most richly decorated in this city.

In 1866, when the dismemberment of the ancient parish of Notre Dame was proclaimed Father Dowd's quick and vigilant eye saw that the congregations of St. Patrick's, and the other Irish churches of this city, would suffer seriously thereby, and he promptly petitioned the Holy See that the Irish Catholics of Montreal should be left in the undisturbed possession of their old privileges; his petition was received and substantially granted, and their position confirmed and defined to their satisfaction.

In 1877 he organized the great Irish Catholic Pilgrimage to Lourdes and Rome. We can all recollect the prayerful anxiety that was felt, when the vessel carrying the pilgrims and their beloved Pastor was not heard of for several agonizing weeks. Prayers were offered in all the churches without distinction of creed, a pleasing proof that we Montrealers are not so bigoted or intolerant as some would make us appear.

When God in great mercy was pleased to restore them to their homes and friends, Father Dowd met with an enthusiastic reception, and was presented with a life-size portrait of himself for the Presbytery of St. Patrick's, where it now hangs.

Father Dowd has, on several occasions, been offered the highest dignities in the church, but has always declined them,—twice at least having refused the mitre, namely :—the Sees of Toronto, and Kingston, Dec. 17, 1852, was named Bishop of Canèe in *partibus*, and Coadjutor of Toronto—declined, preferring to remain with his dear St. Patrick's congregation, to whom he has devoted his life, feeling, as he has always felt, that he could do more good here than he could do elsewhere even though he wore the mitre.

We shall make a few concluding remarks on the leading characteristics for which the Revd. Father Dowd is so noted.

His large and comprehensive views have preserved him from falling into defects common to petty minds. His great intellect never deals with minor difficulties, but grapples only with questions of major importance. He has exhibited in his long career great talent and enterprise in the conception and execution of the various good works referred to above, which stamps his as a master mind. Joined to remarkably deep and profound thoughts is his powerfully persuasive eloquence, whose golden chords have been tuned with exquisite harmony to the highest subjects of religion, not only to St. Patrick's pulpit, but also in Toronto, Kingston, Ottawa and other places in this country and in Ireland, where his brilliant and impressive sermons were greatly admired. His depth of argumentation and his sublimity of expression give way at moments to the charm of gay and innocent conversation. It is chiefly in the exercise of hospitality that the largeness of his Irish heart becomes apparent. His residence is the home of the Irish Ecclesiastic, whether priest or prelate, and while sharing his abundant but frugal repast, his welcome guests have frequently remarked that, "the best sauces served at table were his fatherly smiles and his pleasing anecdotes." The members of the Irish Canadian pilgrimage referred to bear witness to the intense pleasure which his company affords. Most pleasing and fascinating in social circles, he is firm and unbending in the discharge of his pastoral duties, without any exception of persons, and without consulting his own personal interests. He directs his flock with a safe hand, warns his parishioners of any impending dangers, he calms the fears of the agitated mind, consoles the sick, assists the poor, and encourages and comforts pious and fervent souls. Endeared to all, respected and revered by all, his counsels are sought after by large numbers of his fellow citizens, for his knowledge extends through every department of Divine and human science. We may say in truth that the spirit of piety and zeal prevail wherever his advice is taken and practised.

It is impossible in this brief sketch to do full justice to the Rev. Pastor of St. Patrick's ; indeed, to write his memoir in full, since he came to this city in 1848, would be to write the history of the Irish Catholics of Montreal for the last 36 years, so intimately has he been associated with every good and charitable work. We are glad to say, though Father Dowd has reached his 74th year, he still preserves all the features of intellectual youth and enjoys excellent health. We conclude by wishing him continued health and strength to guide and direct the large flock confided to his care.

REV. FATHER JOSEPH TOUPIN.

Rev. Father Joseph Toupin belongs to one of the oldest and most respected French-Canadian families in the province, and was born in Montreal on the 23rd of November, 1814. He was baptized by the Rev. Abbé Bédard in the old Notre Dame Church, and pursued his classical studies at the old Montreal College then on College street. Among his professors were the Abbé Séry, whose memory Father Toupin still cherishes, the Rev. Father Larkin, and the Abbé Roque. The Superiors of the Seminary, who directed him for over fifty years, were the Rev. Abbés Quiblier, Billaudelle, Granet, Bayle, and the present Superior, Abbé Colin.

After a brilliant college course, Father Toupin entered religious orders, receiving the Tonsure and minor orders in 1834 from the hands of Mgr. Lartigue, the first Bishop of Montreal. In 1837 he was successively made sub-deacon and deacon, and finally on the 23rd December, 1837, he was ordained priest. He lost his father in 1834, in the second cholera, and his mother lived until 1857, with another son, the Rev. Alfred Toupin, who was until the time of his death, in 1877, curé of Rivière des Prairies. His only sister married Mr. Lachapelle, and is the mother of the present Doctor Lachapelle.

Father Toupin commenced his ministerial career as professor in the Montreal College, where he taught classics for fifteen years with such success, that up to the present day his name is mentioned in the institution as that of a model professor. Subsequently he was appointed missionary to the Indians at Oka, and after serving there for several years he was called to the city, and has ever since been intimately connected with the several Irish Catholic congregations. He was for many years curé of old St. Bridget's Church, and also of St. Ann's, and was later on attached to St. Patrick's Church, a position which he still holds.

Brotherly love caused Father Toupin temporarily to abandon his work among the Irish people when he went to perform the ministerial duties for his infirm brother, then parish priest at Rivière des Prairies. Immediately after his brother's death, Father Toupin returned to this city with renewed zeal and ardor.

It would be difficult to find a more worthy clergyman than the subject of this brief sketch. Humble and unassuming, Father Toupin has passed his whole life in earnest ministerial work, a slave to duty, and absolutely devoted to those entrusted to his care. Although actively engaged in parochial work, there is hardly a Catholic institution in the whole city which has not been the object of his solicitude, and which he has not helped in some manner. He has been spiritual adviser to several religious communities, who all profess the greatest respect and devotion to him. In his own order, Father Toupin is considered as a model of regularity, and the members of his congregation never found his zeal at fault, being always ready for sick calls, either by day or by night. All these qualities are enhanced by the genial character of this honorable priest, who is always seen with a kind smile on his face, however arduous his duties and great his fatigue may be. It is no wonder that the Irish Catholics of Montreal have a kind of adoration for this devoted priest, who has devoted his life to their welfare.

The following amongst other tributes to the Rev. Fathers Dowd and Toupin appeared in the press of the city.

A DOUBLE PRIESTLY JUBILEE.

There are certain events in the life of every community which seem instinctively to enlist the sympathies of all classes, irrespective of race or creed. Of these is the public tribute about to be paid to the Rev. Messrs. Dowd and Toupin, on the occasion of the fiftieth anniversary of their ordination to the priesthood. The Church of St. Patrick is the focal point around which the interest centres, but that interest impinges from a wide circumference including every province of the Dominion, and a broad range of the United States, wherever Montreal Irish boys have gone forth to face the world, but still remembering the old shrine where they first learned the lessons of life.

The gentlemen of the Seminary, not being members of a religious order, according to strict ecclesiastical nomenclature, but of a congregation, have adopted the title of abbé. The Irish people, however, have not taken to this style, preferring the appellation of "Father," universally employed in the mother land. As applied to Father Dowd, the term is particularly distinctive, meaning exactly what it says. For fifty years he has been a priest according to the order of Melchisedech, and for forty years, during which he has resided consecutively in Montreal, his whole talent, time, energy and health have been devoted to one single object—the good of the people to whom his ministrations were devoted. The details of the career of Father Dowd need not be given here—as they will be rehearsed separately during the celebration—and it will be sufficient to point out the main features of the Jubilee. On Tuesday next, the 17th May, a musical festival will be held in the Queen's hall, under the able direction of St. Patrick's choir, with the distinguished co-operation of such artists as Mrs. Page-Thrower, Mrs. Seymour, Miss Crompton and others. It is intended to make this a characteristic entertainment, and it is to be expected that literature, in the shape of oratory and verse, will have a due part therein.

On Thursday, the 19th inst., the religious ceremony will take place in St. Patrick's church, when appropriate addresses will be read to the two venerable pastors, and a substantial testimonial will be presented to Father Dowd. In this practical age, it is usual to make offerings of this kind take the shape of valuables, and such will be the case on the present occasion. What will render it particularly handsome and significant is the fact that many of the contributors are of a

F

different origin and belief. This circumstance deserves to be specially signalized, and is sure to attract attention abroad. In a community like ours, composed of such diverse elements, the spirit of fellowship, good-will and forbearance is a necessity of existence. As we must live together and have common interests, it is necessary that we should know each other, appreciate each other, and when occasion offers, help each other. Circumstances have of late tended to lessen this temper of mutual conciliation, but Father Dowd's golden jubilee will have the result of uniting us once more. Many Protestant gentlemen have declared their intention of assuming a part in the celebration for this very object, taking advantage of their high personal esteem and respect for the worthy recipient, who himself has been a leading worker to that end during his long pastorate. Father Dowd has always belonged to the good old school of Christian charity, the exponent of honest first principles, and the advocate of every movement looking to the advancement of all classes.

This unanimity of sentiment is the more pleasing that there have been two precedents for the same within the past few years. When Canon Carmichael left us for Hamilton—happily to return as we all hoped and predicted—the Irish Catholics of Montreal came forward spontaneously with a presentation, which the Reverend Dean, Irish-like, at once converted into a cabinet and bookcase to store his Irish library and curiosities. A little later, on the departure of the Rev. Gavin Lang, for Scotland, a similar scene was enacted, and almost the last visit of the Reverend pastor was to Father Dowd.

Another aspect of the Jubilee will be the participation of the French-Canadian people. Not only does Father Dowd belong to a congregation which is of French origin and of which he is a highly honored member, being on the board of the council of the Seminary, but his faithful coadjutor, Rev. M. Toupin, will hold his anniversary at the same time, and share in all the tributes paid to his life-long colleague and friend. Father Toupin belongs to an old and distinguished French family of the Island of Montreal, and having at an early period been placed in contact with the congregation of St. Patrick's, he linked his fortunes with theirs when seemingly better advantages were open to him among his own people. His has been, through all these years, the mission of the modest, unassuming vicar or assistant; but those who know him best can bear testimony to the devotion which has attended all his labors, through the various functions of priestly life, from the baptismal font of the infant, the first communion of the adolescent, the marriage benediction of the young couple, the attendance—day and night—by the sick bed, and the final prayer and requiem at the open grave on Cote des Neiges. It is right of itself, and well for ourselves, that we men of the world should turn aside a moment and show that we can appreciate such qualities and such services. The true clergyman is the highest ideal of manhood, the best guide of the family, and the main prop of that social fabric which must be founded on religious principles. By honoring such men we honor ourselves, and teach our children the ennobling virtue of gratitude.

JOHN LESPERANCE.

Montreal Gazette.

A GLOWING TRIBUTE TO FATHER DOWD FROM REV. GAVIN LANG.

We have great pleasure in publishing the following warm and very complimentary letter of the Rev. Gavin Lang, late minister of St. Andrew's Church of this city, to his friend Mr. Edward Murphy, congratulating the venerable pastor of St. Patrick's Church, Father Dowd, on the occasion of his golden jubilee, which will take place on the 19th inst.

INVERNESS, Scotland, 29th April, 1887.

DEAR MR. MURPHY,—I see, in a recently received Montreal paper, the announcement of an impending celebration in honor and commemoration of the jubilee of the ministry of my old friend and neighbor, Father Dowd, of St. Patrick's Church. In that announcement, it is suggested that there should be an expression of sympathy on the occasion from brother clergymen of all creeds and persuasions. I earnestly hope that this suggestion will be acted upon by Protestants as well as Roman Catholics. Though no longer resident or laboring in Montreal, I feel a strong desire to offer my tribute of respect and best wishes for continued usefulness to the venerable priest, and I can think of no better way of conveying such, in order that they may be added to those of like character, than by asking you, one of his most prominent coadjutors, to do so in the manner and at the time you may think best.

Even the slightest reference to the name of good Father Dowd brings up many and various memories. I had occasion, more than once, to ask his advice upon public questions, and was always received with the most pleasing courtesy. I well remember the

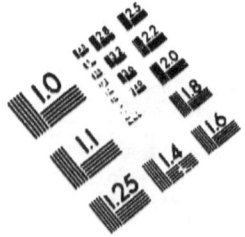

**IMAGE EVALUATION
TEST TARGET (MT-3)**

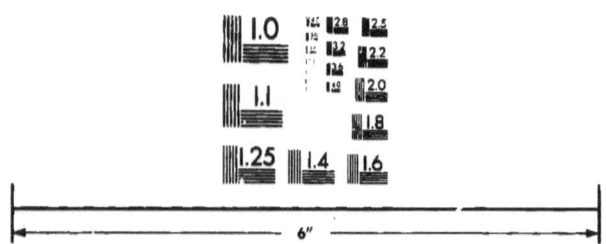

Photographic
Sciences
Corporation

23 WEST MAIN STREET
WEBSTER, N.Y. 14580
(716) 872-4503

time of intense anxiety during the, as was supposed, perilous and
disastrous voyage he made, now many years ago, *en route* to Rome,
and the relief we all—all Montreal and Canada—felt when the news
came that the travellers in the ship had been spoken at sea and no
worse fate had befallen them than the breaking of a shaft. Very
thoughtfully *The Star* sent me a communication of the welcome
tidings to St. Andrew's Church during the service, and, it being
handed up to the pulpit, we joined in giving thanks, then and there,
to Almighty God for his merciful preservation of our fellow citizens.
Nor do I forget the season of suspense caused by an illness through
which Father Dowd passed, and I have the most grateful recollection
of the kind things he said when I left Montreal and returned to
Scotland. Shortly before that, I had been anxious to hear one of
the Redemptorist Fathers preach, and when I was looking about
for a seat, he sent one of his officials to show me to one, which
turned out to be that of my old friend, Dr. Hingston—a courtesy
which was repeated at another service which I attended in St.
Pratrick's on St. Patrick's Day.

You will have many gatherings around Father Dowd, at the
Jubilee celebration to render, in person, their desires for his prolonged
life and increasing happiness. I will be with and of them in heart
and spirit. Even before then, will you give him my kindest regards
and with the same to yourself,

Believe me, yours very faithfully,

GAVIN LANG,

Late Minister of St. Andrew's Church (Church of Scotland), Montreal.

EDW. MURPHY, ESQ., Montreal.

CITY, May 18, 1887.

EDWARD MURPHY, ESQ.,

MY DEAR SIR,—I trust that it will not be intrusive on my part if
I take the freedom of conveying to you, and, by your kindness, to
the Rev. Fathers Dowd and Toupin, whose jubilee of priestly
service will be so justly celebrated to-morrow, the assurance of my
personal interest in so beautiful an occasion. I have not the honor
of acquaintance with either of these reverend gentlemen ; never-
theless, in view of the cordial relations which formerly existed
between the Rev. Dr. Cordner and your honored Pastor, and also
the gratefully remembered fact, that many years ago in a time of

trouble, the Church of the Messiah found a generous friend in Father Dowd—who, I beg to add, is known to me as well as to all our citizens, for his noble character and work, I cannot resist the impulse to join by these words in the general tribute of the morrow.

Both Fathers Dowd and Toupin have rendered eminent service to the cause of religion and the well-being of this City; and I, for my own part, am glad to share the common expression of respectful appreciation. I congratulate you all, that they have reached so honorable a period of clerical usefulness, and most sincerely hope that they may be long spared in health and happiness.

My personal esteem for yourself justifies me in addressing you in these familiar words, and in remaining,

Dear Sir,

Very truly yours,

WM. S. BARNES.

Minister of Church of the Messiah (Unitarian).

Of the many poems written and published in honor of Father Dowd's Jubilee, the following by Miss B. Guerin, of this City, is of the best. It certainly deserves a place in this little volume which we gladly give it.

TO REVEREND FATHER DOWD.

Rejoice! oh rejoice! let our glad voices swelling
With mirth and with music resound on the air!
A sense of delight in each bosom is dwelling,
There are smiles on each lip as it murmurs a prayer—
A heartfelt thanksgiving to God is ascending,
Our joy is the purest that Heaven can send,
While age's weak voice and youth's clear notes are blending
To honor our Pastor, our Father and Friend.

Five decades have passed since with hands consecrated
He took up life's chaplet, and told the first bead,
And still as he numbers them angels elated
Are tracing the record of each noble deed.
Did he see that May morn when he stood at the altar,
This milestone of gold looming out from afar
Through the azure of years, with a flicker and falter,
As dim and mysterious as evening's white star!

That May-day now seems to return, like a vision
Of home and heaven ! He kneels to adore,
But the incense is laden with perfume elysian
Of hawthorn in bloom on his own native shore !
He offers to God his life's vow all unbroken ;
His voice, as in youth, is as ardent and strong,
But while the heart-words with deep reverence are spoken,
He hears once again the lark's tremulous song.

Then memory, aroused, awakes from her slumbers
And shows him the lake-jewelled Island again,
The tear-begemmed Island, and sings in soft numbers
A song of glad youth in an exquisite strain.
But Erin, your charms, though so sweet, did not bind him.
Like his own loved Saint Patrick he heard a low call,
And rising, he left your fair green hills behind him,
Your sea-girdled shore, that bound home, friends and all !

Amongst us he dwelt, and the busy years flying
As noiseless as thistle-down borne on the air,
Wove a crown of love's flowers immortal, undying,
Which to-day on his brow shines above his white hair.
A Patriarch Priest ! lo, he stands in the glory
Of life's setting sun which illumines the west,
And lights with its radiance the whole of life's story,
A gorgeous decline to a day that was blest !

You have known him, oh hearts, that were wounded with sorrow ;
His touch had the magic of exquisite balm.
Oh ! sinners that feared every wakening to-morrow,
His voice has restored you heaven's sunlight and calm.
Ye orphans that mourned for a father and mother,
In him you have found both ; and he labored and strove,
For the home that protects you ; he shared with no other
The right to befriend you, to guard you and love.

For love rises up from his soul like a fountain,
And charity falls like the spray from his hands,
What he holds is all ours, and he claims no amount in,
For poor as the poorest amongst us he stands.
The mitre above his great brow might have glistened ;
The crozier been given him a proud flock to guide,
To the words of his wisdom the wise might have listened,
But still with Christ's little ones he would abide.

Once only he left us— with steps deferential,
He bore to the feet of Christ's vicar on earth,
The homage and love of our hearts reverential ;
Than proudest of treasures to him of more worth,
He gave him the calm and undying assurance
That though the whole world with sedition might ring,
Though wild winds might rage with unswerving endurance,
We cling to our faith and our heaven-crowned King.

Oh ! boundless indeed was our hearts' great emotion,
When weary we waited through long weeks in vain,.
For a word or a sign from the wide-spreading ocear,
To say we should see our dear Father again.
The sun hid its light through these long hours of mourning,
But hope's gentle star through the gloom shed its rays,
Till clouds having passed, the glad sunshine returning,
Awakened our souls to an anthem of praise !

'Round Mary's dear shrine, at each close of day kneeling,
While music arose on the odorous air,
Our hearts with each throb of the organ were feeling
A dread, that found vent in a wild wordless prayer,
A great nameless fear through our bosoms was thrilling,
Lest danger the pilgrim's frail bark should o'erwhelm,
Till from our Queen's heart came a sweet message stilling
Our anguish !—we knew she would watch at the helm.

Oh Father beloved ! thy heart must be swelling
With joy, to remember the things thou hast known—
The Church has twice spoken—its thunder tones telling
That Truth the unerring is ever its own.
Thou hast heard the sweet chant from ten thousand throats springing
Which still day by day is resounded again,
Through all time 'twill be sung—through eternity ringing
Oh ! Mary Immaculate is the refrain

Now on the calm sea of age thou art sailing,
And the silver chord tightens which draws thee to shore,
But the chain of our love is about thee unfailing,
We would hold thee from Heaven—for we need thee still more !
Yes, stay with us, Father, long years—till resembling
The Apostle who loved most and lay on His breast,
And taught His sweet precept—with aged lips trembling :
" Oh ! love ye each other and so be ye blest !"

Thy virtues we hold up to-day to the nation ;
Thy name through our land a glad echo has stirr'd ;
It falls from all lips with a deep veneration,
By the next generation it still will be heard,
It will speak in each stone of St. Patrick's forever,
The temple that thou hast made for us a home—
A monument telling that nothing could sever
Thy love for thy children, for Erin and Rome.]1

THANKS.

The undersigned, in the discharge of a pleasing duty, desire to convey, through the President, their grateful thanks to all their kind friends and generous benefactors, on the occasion of the fiftieth anniversary of their ordination to the priesthood. They beg to present their cordial and respectful acknowledgments to the Archbishops and Bishops, who, at very great inconvenience, were pleased to honor the feast by their presence ; to His Grace the Archbishop of Montreal, who, with extreme goodness, assisted at all the exercises of the day ; to His Grace the Archbishop of Toronto, whose long standing friendship made him forget the pain and fatigue of the journey from Toronto to Montreal ; to His Lordship the Bishop of London, who crowned the occasion by preaching a sermon that will be long remembered ; to His Lordship the Bishop of Peterboro, the respected fellow pilgrim of Father Dowd to Rome ; and also to His Grace Archbishop Taché, who left his sick room to take some part in the proceedings of the day.

They offer affectionate thanks to their brother priests, who came from distant parts of the United States and of the Dominion, as also to those from the city and suburbs of Montreal. Similar thanks are offered to the large number of priests whom the duties of ministry kept away ; we gratefully accept their good wishes and the promise of their prayers.

We owe a special debt of gratitude to our friends outside St. Patrick's Congregation, Catholics and Protestants, who generously contributed to swell the Jubilee fund. Amongst our special benefactors we must name Mr. Notman, who presented each of us with a magnificent life-size portrait. We would be ungrateful did we not acknowledge the very great kindness shown to us by the Press without distinction.

In our inability to write to each, all our dear and respected friends will please accept this assurance of our heartfelt thanks and lasting gratitude.

J. TOUPIN, Ptre.
P. DOWD, Priest.

APPENDIX.

The following report of the proceedings of general and special committees, for the carrying out of the Jubilee celebration, etc., was kindly prepared by W. J. O'Hara, Esq., the indefatigable secretary.

A meeting of the pew holders and congregation generally of St. Patrick's Church, Montreal, was held in the Sacristy after Grand Mass, Sunday, the 11th July, 1886, for the purpose of adopting means to reduce the capital debt of the Church, bearing interest, amounting to $102,000. The total debt is $124,590, but $22,000 due the Seminary being without interest.

The Reverend Father Dowd, Pastor of St. Patrick's, opened the proceedings by explaining the object of the meeting, and submitting, for consideration, the following propositions :—

1. That a subscription list be opened forthwith, the subscription o be paid any time before the 1st May, 1887.

2. That a treasurer be appointed; if desired, the Reverend Father Quinlivan would consent to act as such.

3. That a Committee be appointed to collect funds, the number of the Committee and the mode of collection to be determined by the meeting.

4. That the Priests regularly attached to the St. Patrick's be, *ex officio*, members of the Committee, for the purpose of receiving all contributions brought to the Sacristy or to the Priests' residence.

5. The amount of subscriptions and collections to be handed over to the Rev. Father Dowd, Pastor of St. Patrick's, on some day in May, 1887, to be hereafter fixed.

The Rev. Pastor then retired, and Mr. Edward Murphy was unanimously chosen chairman, and Mr. William J. O'Hara, secretary, of the Congregation Committee, for the purpose of carrying out the object in view.

After some enthusiastic remarks by the Chairman, it was moved by Mr. James O'Brien, seconded by Mr. Owen McGarvey, and unanimously carried, that a subscription list be opened at this meeting for the object in question, and the occasion of the Reverend Father Dowd's fiftieth anniversary of ordination to the priesthood (golden jubilee) selected, as an appropriate one to present to him the amount realized.

A list was accordingly opened, and upwards of $6,000 there and then subscribed.

The Rev. Father Quinlivan was requested to act as Treasurer of the Fund, consented, and received the amount of subscriptions then paid. The meeting then adjourned until the following Sunday.

∗

At the adjourned meeting held at the same time and place, on Sunday, the 18th July, 1886, Mr. Edward Murphy in the Chair, and Mr. O'Hara, Secretary, the Reverend Pastor of St. Patrick's reported additional subscriptions made since the former meeting, amounting to $3,270. Upwards of $650 was subscribed at this meeting, making the total subscription to that date nearly $10,000. Adjournment made until the following Sunday.

∗

At the meeting which was held, on Sunday, the 25th July, 1886, the Reverend Father Dowd, in the absence of Mr. Edward Murphy, took the Chair. A number of subscriptions were reported, and a larger number received at the meeting. After discussion, it was determined to postpone the appointment of a collecting committee until after the summer holidays, many of the Congregation being absent from the city at that time. Whereupon, an adjournment was made until the first Sunday in September.

∗

The meeting appointed for the first Sunday of September, 1886, and postponed in consequence of the Cathedral (St. Peter's) Bazaar, was, after notice from the pulpit, held on Sunday, 28th November, 1886.

The Rev. Father Dowd occupied the Chair. There was a good attendance.

The question of appointing collecting committees to make domiciliary visits, and to take collections at the Church doors on Sundays, was considered, but action in that respect was postponed.

It was deemed expedient to continue for some time longer the Sunday meetings, so as to give every one in the Congregation an opportunity to come forward voluntarily, and add to the Fund. The Rev. Father Dowd was requested to take early opportunity to explain to the Congregation the practical result of lessening the debt by $20,000 or $25,000, thereby saving upwards of $1,000 per annum interest, which could either be used to liquidate so much of the capital annually or to form a sinking fund, which, in time, would liquidate the debt altogether, thus giving hope to the effort to raise that sum. A desire was also expressed that the Reverend Clergy, themselves, take up the monthly Sunday collection in the Church ; and a motion to that effect, proposed by Mr. Edward Murphy, and seconded by Mr. J. J. Curran, was carried unanimously.

A number of subscriptions and payments were reported and made, and the meeting adjourned.

***

At the adjourned meeting held on Sunday, the 12th December, 1886, the Reverend Father Dowd occupied the Chair.

Subscriptions were reported and payments made ; and upon motion of Dr. W. H. Hingston, seconded by Mr. Edward Murphy, it was unanimously resolved that a circular be prepared by the Rev. Father Dowd, and sent to all those from whom a subscription was expected, the circular to be submitted at next meeting.

***

The Circular was submitted at the next meeting, Sunday, 19th December, 1886, by the Rev. Father Dowd, and approved. A few subscriptions were received, and adjournment was made until after the Christmas and New-Year Holidays.

***

The next meeting was held on Sunday, the 27th March, 1887, the Treasurer, Rev. Father Quinlivan, in the absence of the Chairman, Mr. Edward Murphy, occupied the Chair, Mr. William J. O'Hara acting as Secretary. After receiving payments and taking new subscriptions, it was resolved that the Reverend Pastor of St. Patrick's, in conjunction with the Rev. Treasurer of this Fund, be requested to appoint a Committee to make domiciliary visits to the parishioners of St. Patrick's and others, for the purpose of soliciting subscriptions to the Fund ; but, before the Committee begin their visits, a circular in form suggested be sent by the Rev. Father Dowd to all from whom contributions were expected, and a short period allowed for spontaneous compliance with the appeal. A form of circular and of subscription note for enclosure therewith was submitted. Quite a number of subscriptions, made since the last meeting in December, 1886, were reported. It was suggested that a meeting of the Congregation generally, to consider the preparations necessary for the due celebration of the Jubilee of the Reverend Fathers Dowd and Toupin, be called for Easter Sunday, after Grand Mass.

***

ST. PATRICK'S CHURCH DEBT.

An Affectionate Appeal to the Parishioners and Friends of St. Patrick's to join in an Effort to Reduce the Debt on that Church:

This appeal is based on the following reasons:

1st. The capital of its debt is the exact cost of the building of St. Patrick's Church, namely, $124,390.

2nd. Of that amount $102,390 bears interest at 4½ per cent., amounting yearly to $4,607.55.

3rd. The remaining $22,000, lent by the Seminary of Montreal, does not bear interest.

4th. When the amount due to the Fabrique of Notre Dame, viz.: $102,390, is paid, principal and interest, the St. Patrick's Church, with the grounds attached, and all dependencies, becomes by the fact the property of the St. Patrick's Parish.

5th. The interest now paid will, in a little over twenty-two years, equal the entire capital of the debt bearing interest, viz.: $102,390; every dollar paid on the capital of the debt diminishes that yearly interest.

6th. Twenty thousand dollars of the capital debt paid reduces the yearly interest by $900.00. Twenty-five thousand dollars paid on same capital debt would reduce the yearly interest by $1,125.00.

7th. It is believed that by a generous and united effort twenty-five thousand dollars can be subscribed, and paid in before the middle of May next; the amount already subscribed by only one hundred and one members of the congregation is over $10,800.

8th. What is saved by reducing the yearly interest goes at once to reduce yet further the capital debt.

9th. If the good will of the parishioners is seriously enlisted in this grand movement, no doubt God will open new sources of revenue by inspiring many to remember the church of their dear Apostle when making their last will, and preparing for eternity.

Montreal, Dec. 18th, 1886.

P. DOWD, Priest.

MEETINGS *IN RE* THE JUBILEE CELEBRATION.

The St. Patrick's Congregation held a meeting in the Sacristy, after Grand Mass, on Sunday, the 17th April. 1887, to consider, and prepare for the celebration, in a fitting manner, of the Golden Jubilee of Reverend Fathers Dowd and Toupin. Mr. Edward Murphy was requested to take the Chair, and Mr. William O'Hara to act as secretary. The leading members of the Congregation were present. It was unanimously resolved upon motion of Dr. Hingston, seconded by Mr. M. P. Ryan, that the Jubilee be celebrated in the following manner :—

1st. That an address in the name of the Congregation be presented to the Reverend Fathers Dowd and Toupin on the occasion.

2. That the address to the Reverend Father Dowd, Pastor of St. Patrick's, be accompanied by a presentation.

3. That the occasion be also celebrated by a banquet.

4. That the members of the Congregation, who can do so, offer private hospitality to the visiting clergy and others.

5. That Committees be named to carry out the foregoing.

The following Committee was appointed to draw up the addresses :—Messrs. Edward Murphy (Chairman), W. H. Hingston, M.D., J. J. Curran, LL.D., Q.C., M.P., Dennis Barry, B.C.L., Alderman W. H. Cunningham, M. J. F. Quinn, Honorable James McShane, Owen McGarvey, James O'Brien, and William J. O'Hara, Secretary.

The Hospitality Committee was constituted as follows : Messrs. M. P. Ryan, J. H. Semple, John McIntyre and Walter Kavanagh, with power to add to their number.

The announcement by the Secretary (Mr. O'Hara) that the choir of St. Patrick's proposed to add to the celebration a Musical Festival, to be held in the Queen's Hall, on the 17th May next, under the auspices of gentlemen of the Congregation, the proceeds of which to be devoted to the Jubilee Fund, was received with pleasure. A Committee, composed of Messrs. John B. Murphy, Bernard Tansey, Bernard Emerson, J. Connaughton, and John Fallon to procure Medals or Badges and Photographs for the celebration, to be sold for the benefit of the Fund, was appointed, and the meeting adjourned.

⁎

At the adjourned meeting held on Sunday, April 24th, Mr. Edward Murphy, Chairman,—reports were received from the

different Committees. A number of names were added to the list
of those offering hospitality to visitors. At this meeting exhaustive
consideration was given to the details of the celebration, and provisions made for carrying out the same with suitable *éclat*. Steps
were taken to afford outside citizens (citizens not members of the
Congregation of St. Patrick's) an c pportunity to join in the
celebration, as a desire to share in the tribute of respect to the
beloved Pastor of St. Patrick's had been generally evinced by the
citizens.

**

Another meeting was held of the Congregation of St. Patrick's on
Sunday, the 1st May, 1887. Mr. Edward Murphy in the Chair, at
which the reports of the various Committees were considered and
approved. A draft of the address to Rev. Father Dowd was
submitted and approved, and the Chairman (Mr. Edward Murphy),
Dr. W. H. Hingston, and the Secretary(Mr. O'Hara) were appointed
a sub-committee to complete the addresses.

Mr. W. H. Cunningham was added to the Committee on Badges,
etc., as Chairman in the absence of Mr. John B. Murphy. It was
resolved that Mr. John B. Murphy's suggestion as to the publication
of a pamphet commemorative of the festival be approved, to be
carried out after the event, unless it be found practicable to have it
ready for the occasion itself.

Mr. M. P. Ryan was appointed Treasurer to receive subscriptions
from persons outside the Congregation, who had shown a disposition
to join in the testimonial to the Reverend Father Dowd, and the
meeting adjourned until the 8th idem.

**

The meeting of the 8th May was entirely taken up with details of
the Jubilee celebration. It was arranged that the addresses be
presented in the church, members of the Temperance Society to act
as ushers and preserve order, the pewholders being requested to
place seats at their disposal for the accommodation of strangers.

The draft of the address to Rev. Father Toupin was read by
Dr. Hingston and approved.

Adjournment was made to the following Sunday.

**

At the meeting, held on Sunday, 15th May, to make final arrangements for the Jubilee celebration, Mr. Edward Murphy occupied

the chair. The Rev. Father Quinlivan, Treasurer, rep·rted the subscriptions and amount paid up to date, of the Jubilee Fund, viz. : Subscriptions $14,772 ; payments $13,648.

Mr. M. P. Ryan (Special Treasurer) reported subscriptions received from persons outside the Congregation, and read a number of friendly communications received in connection therewith, amongst others from:—The Reverend Father Catulle, Pastor of St. Ann's ; Mr. James F. Black, City Treasurer ; Mr. John Crawford of Verdun ; Very Rev. Dean Carmichael ; Mr. W. S. Goodhue.

The Chairman (Mr. Edward Murphy) read a letter from the Rev. Gavin Lang, late Minister of St. Andrew's Church, Montreal, now of Inverness, Scotland, who spoke in the kindliest manner of Father Dowd as his " dear old friend and neighbor."

It was arranged as to the presentation of addresses that precedence be given to the representative of the Federal Government, the Honorable Mr. Thompson, Minister of Justice, who had kindly, signified his intention of being present, to be followed by the Corporation of Montreal. Next in order, the address of the Congregation to the Rev. Father Dowd to be read by Mr. Edward Murphy, Chairman, an⁴ the address to Rev. Father Toupin to be read by Dr. W. H ı ton. Rev. Father Quinlivan to follow with the address of ₐₗ Ladies of the Congregation, and the remaining addresses in the order announced from the pulpit that day.

Arrangement was made for a platform from which to read the addresses, and the meeting adjourned.

There were several informal meetings of sub-committees prior to the celebration, to complete arrangements for the successful carrying out of the same.

At a meeting of the Congregation held after the Jubilee, to wit :—on Sunday, the 29th May, 1887, after Grand Mass, in the Sacristy, to receive reports of the same and wind up the business connected therewith. Mr. Edward Murphy occupied the chair, and there was a large attendance. Report was received of the expenses of the celebration in the Church, viz: Decorations $75, Music $52, Printing, etc., $36.18, total $163.18. The Reverend Treasurer,

Father Quinlivan, reported the result of the Jubilee Fund collection
as follows:—

The Congregation generally....... ....$16,593 44

From Societies :--

St. Patrick's Society......................................	100	00
St. Patrick's Choir..	320	00
St. Patrick's School (past and present pupils)..	365	co
The Ladies of Charity of the Congregation and their friends......	1000	00
Society of the Living Rosary...................	251	25
Catholic Young Men's Society.......................	205	00
The Leo Club.....	106	49
The Catechism Children.....................	525	00
St. Patrick's Temperance Society	500	00
The Children of Mary Society.......................	201	50
St. Patrick's Orphans.......	50	00
Catholic friends.............................	387	00

4,011 24

$20,604 68

After considering reports of the Badge and Photograph Committee, the question of the publication of the pamphlet, comme
morative of the occasion, was discussed, and it was resolved that
the pamphlet be prepared and published, containing :—

1. An historical account of the Church (St. Patrick's) and its
associations, its early pastors, etc., and other matters of interest in
connection with the early religious history of the Irish Catholic
people of Montreal.

2. An account of the Charitable and Educational Establishments
connected with and surrounding the Church.

3. Biographical sketches of the Reverend Fathers Dowd and
Toupin.

4. Account of the Jubilee Celebration in its various parts, the
Musical Festival, the School Celebration, the religious celebration,
the sermon of the day, the banquet, the addresses, poems, etc., etc.

5. A list of subscribers to the Fund, and such other matters as
the Committee may see fit and appropriate.

The following gentlemen were appointed a committee to have the
pamphlet compiled and published, viz.:—Rev. Father Quinlivan,

Mr. Edward Murphy (Chairman), Dr. W. H. Hingston, J. J. Curran, LL.D., Q.C., M.P., William J. O'Hara (Secretary), Dennis Barry, B.C.L., and Bernard Emerson.

This Committee arranged to meet the following Tuesday, and the meeting adjourned.

*_**

The sub-committee met on Tuesday, 31st May, 1887, and arranged the subject matter of the pamphlet, which it was found could be most satisfactorily published by Messrs. John Lovell & Son.

*_**

The sub-committee appointed to prepare and publish the Jubilee Pamphlet Souvenir met on Sunday, the 18th September, 1887.

There were present: Rev. Father Quinlivan, Messrs. Edward Murphy (Chairman), J. J. Curran, Dennis Barry, B. Emerson, and William O'Hara (Secretary).

Mr. J. J. Curran read the Introductory or Prefatory Chapter written by him for the Jubilee pamphlet, and submitted a sketch of the subject matter, its compilation and arrangement. A resolution expressing the approval and appreciation of the Committee therewith, and without delay, in favor of the publication of the Jubilee pamphlet, as prepared under the editorship of Mr. Curran, was passed unanimously.